OTHER BOOKS BY RICHARD PECK AVAILABLE IN
LAUREL-LEAF BOOKS:

ARE YOU IN THE HOUSE ALONE?
BEL-AIR BAMBI AND THE MALL RATS
DON'T LOOK AND IT WON'T HURT
PRINCESS ASHLEY
REMEMBERING THE GOOD TIMES
SECRETS OF THE SHOPPING MALL

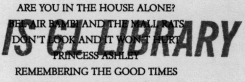

The

Last

Safe

Place

on

EARTH

RICHARD PECK

LAUREL-LEAF BOOKS

Published by
Bantam Doubleday Dell Books for Young Readers
a division of
Bantam Doubleday Dell Publishing Group, Inc.
1540 Broadway
New York, New York 10036

Material from *Fahrenheit 451* by Ray Bradbury reprinted by kind permission of Don Congdon Associates, Inc.

ISBN: 0-440-22007-6

RL: 5.5

Reprinted by arrangement with Delacorte Press

Printed in the United States of America

August 1996

10   9   8   7

OPM

for

Susan
Stevens

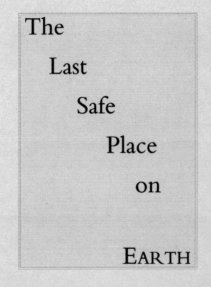

The

Last

Safe

Place

on

EARTH

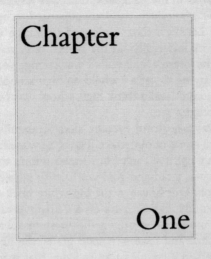

Chapter

One

Halloween's a week and a half away, Homecoming the weekend after. It's that time of year and coming home, I'm thinking: What a great evening to be going somewhere with a girl—my arm draped over her soft shoulder, the two of us scuffing through the leaves. I'm seeing girls everywhere I look, some of them real, most not. I see girls in the shapes the tree trunks make and in the formations of the clouds. I see a lot of girls this fall. I'm not obsessed. I'm in tenth grade.

So I was coming home on foot. There were a couple of books in my backpack. One was Ray Bradbury's *Fahrenheit 451,* which we were supposed to be reading for Mrs. Lensky's class. I planned to buckle down on schoolwork and really hit the books, next year, senior year at the latest. Meanwhile I was taking every day as it came, trying to get a toehold on high school. But the fact is, I didn't really think high school was happening until I found a girl.

It was a postcard evening along Tranquillity Lane, the actual name of our street. The haze was like bonfire smoke, though we can't burn leaves within the village limits. It was a red-and-gold world with purple evening coming on. Our house is the big white brick with the green shutters, like a house on a Christmas card.

We used to live out in the western suburbs. But when Diana and I were in sixth grade, the junior high out there had a couple of knife fights that made news. The gangs were moving in, so we moved out.

Also, Dad got a promotion around then. I'm not that clear about what a vice-president in mortgage banking does, except that Dad says practically everybody he knows is one. When we were in grade school they had this deal where dads took their daughters to work with them for a day. It was so girls wouldn't feel left out about careers, so Dad took Diana to the bank. But they never had a day for sons.

So when I was twelve we moved to Walden Woods—for the schools, the way people do. It looked good to me. It looked like a place without any surprises. And I guess you could say it was pretty much perfect, the last safe place on earth. I turned into our drive and did the last lap at my usual speed.

As a family we eat an unusual number of meals together. I slid out of my backpack and warm-up jacket to find Dad already in the kitchen. He's six foot three, so I may top out around there. A can of Coors was on the table in front of him with the top popped. He was in his captain's chair, examining some new leaf-raking blisters on the heel of his hand.

I swung in, running an offhand hand through my damp hair. I'd made sophomore swim team, a very respectable alternative to going out for JV football. And I liked to keep my hair wet a lot of the time just to make the point.

"Hey, Dad. Beer looks good. Think I'll have one."

"In about six years," he said, hoisting his brew to toast me. "Did I ever tell you what happened when your grandpa Tobin caught me smoking a Marlboro in eleventh grade?"

"Did it involve having to paint the whole house, Dad?"

"Two coats."

Dad was in his yard-work mode: a sweatshirt reading WALDEN WOODS WARRIORS that happened to be mine, a pair of Kelly-green sweatpants that were all his, and his lucky gym shoes. Whole parts of him have never really matured.

But I gave him high marks as a dad. He even liked yard work, especially after racquetball ruined his hamstrings for running. And fall's his favorite time of year, so he signed up voluntarily on the family roster for raking. He said it got the kinks out after a day at the bank. I encouraged this. He'd stopped raking halfway across the front lawn, but I was willing to let that pass.

"I didn't get much done this evening," he said, fingering a blister. "Why are we out of leaf bags?"

"Are they on the list?"

"No, because I didn't think we were running low. What are you doing with the leaf bags, Todd?"

Dad's got a lot of little trick questions like that, and I used to fall for them, but not so much anymore. "Dad, trust me. I stay as far from leaf bags as I can."

"That's what I thought too." He took a swig. "But then I had this idea you might be smuggling them to school to drop over girls' heads, hoping to bag a date."

"I can see how you might think that, Dad. But let me put you in the picture. At Walden Woods we're too cool to 'date,' whatever that might mean. Hey, I'm on the swim team. I'm the one who ought to get bagged."

"You remind me a lot of myself at your age," he remarked. "But next time don't take any more leaf bags than you need." Then Dad's big finish: "Leaf bags don't grow on trees, you know."

I was already turning to consult the refrigerator, where we hang our weekly rosters. The refrigerator door's covered with Marnie's Sunday School artwork under magnets, going back two years to kindergarten. It's mostly crayon pictures of the sun rising over our house and all of us standing out in Tranquillity Lane with big grins: Dad, Mom, Diana and me, Marnie—and we're all the same size.

My fourth-grade school picture is still up there on display, too, and so is Diana's. I look like a nine-year-old chipmunk. Diana looks deadly serious, like she's being booked for a juvenile crime. We didn't live here when those pictures were taken. Mom shifted them from one refrigerator to another in the move. There's even a picture of her and Dad before they were married, and they've both got very strange haircuts. Dad says he met Mom at a Stones concert, which she denies. But they must have met in college. There's a yearbook up in the attic, and they're both in it. The refrigerator pictures were all curling, but we didn't touch them. Mom has a sentimental streak.

Around on the side of the refrigerator the rosters hung under more magnets. We had lists and assignments for everything: meals, chores, supplies, you name it. Since we were all on different schedules, we were organized down to a nanosecond around here. Tonight Marnie and I were in charge of cooking.

I was cool. When it was my cooking night, we had beanie-weenie, and I stockpiled the ingredients for it. Marnie was down for the salad.

I buy my baked beans by the case, and I get the regular store brand—Jewel. Beans are beans, so why pay extra? I was showing Dad how I can juggle three sixteen-ounce cans when we heard Mom's car in the drive. Three cans will serve five people unless that's all you're having.

By the time I had the lids off the beans and had pried the weenies out of the freezer, we heard Diana coming in the front door. I had the weenies on to boil and was digging around for two medium-size onions or one big one when a strange small shape streaked into the kitchen.

It was Marnie, who'd just remembered she was salad. She wore half her costume for upcoming Halloween. It was a witch's rig and probably meant to be in tatters anyway. But right now it was only half made. With the witch skirt she was wearing a cotton top from Gap Kids. Because she was seven, every tooth in her head was a different size, with one missing in front. This carried out the witch theme. Since she was serious about everything, she wanted to have her salad down cold before Mom and Diana appeared. She's the baby, so she has a lot of catch-up ball to play.

Paying Dad and me no attention, she turned on a dime on the way to the refrigerator. By then I had on the swimmer's goggles I keep in the knife drawer. I wear goggles for peeling and dicing onions. Call me crazy, but it's better than crying in your onions.

Behind me Marnie the witch was advancing with her salad. It was bound to be Jell-O. She loves Jell-O. I had my beans in a bowl by then and a Corning Ware casserole dish out and greased. I caught a glimpse of Marnie from the side of my goggle as she bustled up to the counter with her salad mold in both hands. She was wearing a single hoop earring of Mom's. The counter's a little high for her anyhow. Then it happened.

She caught one sneaker in her witch skirt, turned in a tangle, and threw the Jell-O mold against the wall. She didn't mean to. It just got away from her and went ballistic. Somehow the Jell-O itself orbited out of the mold in midflight. The mold bounced down in the sink, clanging like a bell. And there was this ring of Jell-O sliding down the tiled wall. It was red, so it was either strawberry or cherry.

"Quick," Marnie screamed. "Get plates!"

Like we were all supposed to serve ourselves salad before it reached the countertop. She'd really worked on it too. There were grapes coming down the wall and banana slices and pineapple chunks. By then I was trying to get ketchup into my beans, but the sight of this Jell-O Niagara distracted me.

Mom and Diana had both appeared in the kitchen door. Mom's hand was over her mouth; Diana's was on a hip. She observed the scene. Marnie in shock and a witch's skirt, with her eyes beginning to fill up. Me in goggles adding a dash of Worcestershire sauce to my beans. Dad in a bad outfit gazing amazed at the Jell-O sinking like a sunset down the wall.

"I'd like to think I've come to the wrong house," Diana said. "But this could only be ours."

We had a simple green salad with the beanie-weenie that night. Some people chop up the weenies and mix them in with the beans. I don't. I boil them till they're fat. Then I fork them out of the water, split their middles open, and add finger-length slices of Cheddar cheese, extra sharp. I distribute the weenies over the top of the casserole. Then, pow, into the microwave for a nuking. They were especially good that night, and we followed up with a Mrs. Smith's pumpkin pie and Cool Whip.

Dad said that a simple green salad was the perfect

complement to my beanie-weenie. Mom ate with one
arm along the back of Marnie's chair. But Marnie didn't
see why we couldn't eat her Jell-O anyway, though the
main clump of it had ended up behind the breadbox,
which doesn't get cleaned on a daily basis. In spite of a
quick sponging, traces of it were still on the wall, too,
like a finger painting. But she'd put a lot into that Jell-O,
and here at the table she was right on the verge. Her
emotions were pretty wobbly anyway. She cried at car-
toons. She was still wearing her witch's skirt and re-
fused to blame it.

Marnie was moping for another reason. We were
having a quick meal because we all had somewhere
else to be, except for her. Mom's club of women runs a
resale clothing shop, and she'd just come home from
there. Now she and Dad were going to get dressed up
to go into the city for some bank-related event. Diana
and I were both going back to school. She was on the
newspaper, and they were putting their Homecoming
issue to bed that night. I was a sophomore rep for the
Homecoming bonfire committee. How I'd gotten that
honor I don't even remember. We were all cutting out,
all but Marnie.

When Diana and I were in junior high, there was
usually somebody at home for her. But now we were
out a lot, in fact as much as possible. After I got
through Driver's Ed, my favorite class, and had my license, I planned to be out even more. I probably didn't
think enough about Marnie. There was that long eight
years between us.

According to Mom, the baby-sitter was somebody

named Laurel Kellerman, which rang no bells with me. "Who is she?" Diana asked.

"Harriet Padgett on my committee recommended her. She lives next door to the Padgetts on High-meadow." Then Mom said to Marnie, "She sounded nice on the phone. Maybe she'll help you work on your Halloween costume."

Marnie wanted sequins and beads and rhinestone cobwebs on her costume. She'd been gluing stuff on it for days, and you'd find these little glittery things around on the floor everyplace. She wanted to be some kind of designer witch.

I only picked up the general trend of this conversation, and Marnie didn't look too sure. She and I loaded the dishwasher. In the background Dad had his thumbs tucked into his sweatpants, saying, "Another fine gourmet meal. You couldn't get a meal like that in a restaurant."

In the scramble to go out again I happened to be the one to hear the bell. When I opened the front door, a car was gliding away from the curb, and there stood Laurel Kellerman. My world lurched.

All my fantasies combined into this perfect girl standing there. My age, maybe. I didn't know. She had a mature look. But Diana always said girls are more mature than guys. She might be right. I might be too immature to know.

"Is this the Tobins'?" she said.

"Yeah," I said. "Really." She wasn't wearing any makeup. She didn't need it. She had on just this blouse with a sweater over her shoulders, and a skirt instead of jeans. Not preppie. Light-years away from grunge. Not trying too hard. Just kind of perfect.

"I'm supposed to baby-sit Marnie," she said.

"Yeah," I said. "Sure." She was thin, but not anorexic or anything. Tallish. Not gawky. She'd never been gawky. She had a book bag on a strap, but she didn't fiddle with it. She was completely composed. I really admire that. You couldn't imagine this girl ever giggling, no matter what.

"Can I come in?" she asked. She was smiling, almost laughing. I wondered what her laugh would sound like. She had good teeth. Excellent teeth. Excellent everything. Why was I barring the door? Why did I step on my own foot when I got out of her way?

seemed to know everybody else. Working real hard to be noticed without being different—and a bit jumpy around all these strangers.

But I was beginning to go with the flow and move with the mass. And I figured I was reasonably normal. All I wanted was to belong and be older, which seemed to be what everybody else wanted too.

Our house was only six blocks from school. Three blocks to Founders Park, a leafy square with big houses around it, then three blocks more. Close enough to walk, far enough to drive when I could. Then when we got to school, it was completely lit up, and the parking lot was full. They've got activities and evening adult-ed classes and open gym and anything you can think of. They call it "Quality Education for a Quality Community." Diana and I went our separate ways after making a plan to walk home together.

The bonfire committee met in the library, and the librarian was Mrs. Noyes. We'd met her during orientation. She wore glasses on a chain and, like Dad, a Walden Woods Warriors sweatshirt. She was transferring books onto a cart under some posters. One was for an upcoming AIDS Awareness meeting they were going to have in the library. Another one, green, seemed to be about ecology. It read:

A CLEANER ENVIRONMENT BEGINS WITH YOUR ROOM

And a big bright one said:

A MIND IS LIKE A PARACHUTE
IT ONLY WORKS WHEN IT'S OPEN

"Bonfire committee?" she said, looking up. "Sophomore?"

I stood taller. "Does it show?"

She grinned. "Not really, but sophomores are always early. Juniors plan to be late, and seniors hold back the longest to make an entrance."

"Ah," I said, trying to look like I knew this. "Are you like the committee advisor?"

"Please. Do I look like I need another job? I'm just trying to keep ahead of these books. During the day I get to be librarian. In the evening I get to be my own assistant." She dumped a pile of paperbacks into my hands. "Here, you can help. Just take them down there to Leisure Reading and put them in the revolving rack. Any order."

So the next person into the library caught me being a library helper, shelving books. That person was Charles Evans Van Meter.

"Sophomore?" Mrs. Noyes inquired as he drifted past her. Yes, but he wasn't on the bonfire committee or any other committee. He'd been my best friend since seventh grade. We'd hung in there together through the worst of puberty. And he'd turned up tonight because I was here and because he seemed to have a lot of free time.

I'd thought being cool meant not noticing every little thing. C. E. Van Meter was born beyond cool. He was round and getting rounder. He walked like a duck and wore sweatshirts with attached drawstring hoods that turned him into a gnome. His family lived in the tackiest house in town. His dad played golf on the pro circuit and regularly lost. His mother drank and called him "Chucky." And the point is: nothing ever seemed to bother him, not even the sight of me sticking paperbacks into the revolving rack.

"C.E.," I said, "are you the other grunt committee rep and I didn't know it?" On cue the other rep from our class entered the library, a bouncy type named Misty, who carried a pink clipboard.

Settling at a long table C.E. stroked his chin and gazed around at the book-lined walls. "What do they call this place?" he said.

When the two junior reps, both girls, turned up, clipboard Misty moved over to them. One of the juniors was Tara Lawrence, but I didn't know that till later. Now the committee's faculty advisor, Mrs. Dalbey, was here. She was a tense woman who taught keyboarding in computer science. I didn't know her age. She was just sort of a teacher's age. Come to think of it, she'd already saved my skin.

I met her during registration. A glitch developed in my printout, scheduling me into three different history classes, four sessions of something called "Music Theory," and no lunch. I was on the edge of freaking out when she came up on me quietly and ran me through the computer again until I got a fairly sane schedule.

Mrs. Dalbey carried a clipboard, too, but hers fluttered with notes. Then the seniors made their entrance.

By law we were two reps from each class, six around the table. But seniors don't move in groups that small. They were a party of six by themselves. There were some major names among them—Steve Inge for one and Boomer Holmberg. I'd seen one of the girls before, Jennifer Wynn. She had a lot of visibility and a lot more eyeliner than you see around Walden Woods. She was basically pretty cheap looking.

The rest of them had their image nailed: a modified stud-and-leather look with some nice layering. And they gave out the impression that they were just passing through on the way to someplace more important. Boomer and three others didn't sit down at all. They lounged against the card catalog. Jennifer Wynn was their spokeswoman, because she sat down at the head of the table. After general introductions Mrs. Dalbey started through our agenda.

The bonfire was going to be on the Saturday night after the game. Apparently we had nothing to do with it. Any bonfire on school property was completely in the hands of the Walden Woods village fire department.

But there'd be a hospitality tent with refreshments, where students and alums could mingle before the bonfire and the dance. Mrs. Dalbey droned, and my mind wandered to the next table, where C.E. was impersonating a library user. He'd picked a paperback from my rack and was reading it upside down, in case anybody noticed.

I'd already decided I wasn't cut out for committee work when Jennifer Wynn's voice interrupted Mrs. Dalbey.

"I don't see why we're even wasting our time with this so-called hospitality tent. Who'll use it? I mean, this is a social occasion, so people want a drink, right?"

She gave Mrs. Dalbey that big-eyed stare girls give to teachers they're trying to bring down.

But underage drinking and drinking on school property are illegal, which Mrs. Dalbey pointed out. Anyway, we had nothing to do with the tent either. It was being donated rent free by Shore Tent & Awning.

"Hypocrites," Jennifer Wynn said. "I am so sick of the hypocrisy of this place."

She was playing to the other seniors. The four standing were all guys, taking their cues from her. My mind wandered again, and now I noticed Steve Inge wasn't by the card catalog anymore. He was over by Tara Lawrence's chair, and I hadn't seen him make his move. I'd noticed Tara around, and not just because she was a year older. She was pretty in that way girls are when they don't know it. Now Steve Inge's hand was on the back of her chair. I couldn't see his hand, but it was there. *So that's how you do it,* I thought, not knowing how he'd done it.

He had a schoolwide reputation with girls. I'd watched him work the school halls and the way he pushed back a girl's hair to whisper something in her ear. He could own girls by looking at them.

The meeting lumbered on and wound down. We got various assignments. By the end Mrs. Dalbey's lips looked thinner. The seniors left first in a bloc, and Tara was with Steve. He'd locked her with his eyes, and she'd walked away from the other junior rep. Misty left, too, and C.E. returned his paperback. Mrs. Noyes was still at the counter as we went by.

"You run a first-rate library operation here," C.E. told her.

Mrs. Noyes rolled her eyes at him, this middle-aged Hobbit, and said, "Tell your friends about us."

We met up with Diana out in the main hall as school was shutting down and people were streaming out. Diana was taller than C.E., but he didn't mind that either. "Who's for a pizza?" he said.

"C.E., it's a school night," Diana said, rolling her eyes.

He blinked at this information and wandered off into the night.

At home a car was parked at the front curb with somebody in it. Inside, Marnie was already in bed, and Laurel Kellerman was doing homework at the end of our dining-room table. The chandelier caught the lights in her hair. The way she wore it was younger than the rest of her. You could imagine a plastic barrette in it. When we came in, she was packing up her book bag. In front of her was a world-history book, tenth grade.

"You're a grunt?" I blurted. "I mean a sophomore? Tenth grade? I thought maybe you were older."

"Give me time," she said, smiling.

"But you didn't go to Ridpath for junior high." Believe me, I'd have remembered her.

"We just moved here this year," she said, "at the beginning of summer."

"We moved here for junior high. Diana and I are tenth grade too."

"I know," Laurel said. "Marnie filled me in." She

and Diana seemed to exchange smiles while I processed this information. Laurel was on her feet now. "Marnie's great. She wanted to watch a movie, but I read to her instead, and we talked. We had a nice time. I'm always available."

"Then do you want to go to the Homecoming bonfire and dance with me?" I said. "It wouldn't be a date. I'm on the committee."

Laurel's hand covered another smile. "I mean I'm always available for baby-sitting."

I felt my entire head go red, but Laurel was saying, "I better go. My dad's outside, waiting." She moved like a dancer, and my mouth was running wild.

"Wait. I'll walk you out to the car."

"It's okay," she said. Then she was gone, leaving this space in the air where she'd been.

I thought Diana was going to take pity on me and not say anything. That would have been truly mature of her. In fact, she didn't speak, but her mouth moved. I could read her lips: *It wouldn't be a date. I'm on the committee.*

"My technique with girls needs work," I said.

"Work?" Diana said. "It needs government funding."

By the time Mom and Dad came home, I was upstairs, somewhat restless. I even thought about cleaning out under my bed, but got a grip on myself. When I couldn't sleep, I reached for the book we were supposed to be reading in Mrs. Lensky's class, the Ray Bradbury book. I flipped it open at random and read,

They walked in the warm-cool blowing night on the silvered pavement and there was the faintest breath of fresh apricots and strawberries in the air, and he looked around and realized this was quite impossible so late in the year.

And it was like I was saying these words, and this is what the day had meant.

In the middle of the night I was suddenly awake. Light from the streetlamp wavered across my bed. The ivy rattled on the outside walls. Then there was a high-pitched scream like the one that must have jolted me out of a dream I couldn't remember. The scream cut through the house. Marnie.

The hall light went on as I got my door open. Mom was pulling her robe around her, going into Marnie's room. Marnie was sobbing—dry, hiccuping sobs. Things scared her sometimes—something she'd see on TV and couldn't let go of. The world could be a scary place to Marnie, but she didn't have too many bad dreams, not that I knew of. I stood there asleep on my feet. Then I turned back to bed because Mom was dealing with it.

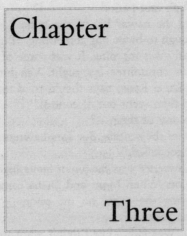

Chapter

Three

We didn't manage breakfasts together. Dad was out of the house before six-thirty for the train into town. Marnie didn't have to be at school till nine. Diana likes toast-on-the-run. I believe in a big breakfast: Eggos, cereal, whatever I find. I was just easing down at the kitchen table when the phone rang.

"This is C. E. Van Meter."

This is the way he always announced himself on the phone, though with that voice, who else could it be? He never called before school. He was usually in a coma through first period.

"Heard the news? It's on the radio." He sounded serious enough to be pulling something. "Big wreck last night or early this morning. It was some of those people on your committee last night. Van hit a tree on Lombardy Lane. Radio says they'd tried to ram a cop cruiser and then went out of control."

"Were any of them—"

"None of the seniors. But Tara Lawrence was with them. She got killed."

Tara Lawrence was the junior Steve Inge had made his moves on. When Mom and Diana came in, I was still collapsing the aerial on the phone. "Was it for me?" Diana asked.

"No, it was C.E." But I didn't want to tell her in front of Mom. I don't know why. Mom was going to find out anyway. But they both saw something in my face.

"You know Tara Lawrence?" I asked Diana.

"Not personally. She's a junior."

"Not anymore." Which was a fairly crude way of leading into C.E.'s news.

Mom was dressed, but she still had her bedroom slippers on. She looked paler and younger, especially after she heard about the accident. And she'd been up in the night with Marnie. "I'll drive you two to school," she said.

"Why?" Diana said.

Mom looked around the kitchen for an answer. "I

don't know why," she said, snapping a little. "Why not?"

Somebody's kid in the community had been killed, and Mom was closing in to protect us.

"Listen, Mom," Diana said in her most reasonable voice. "It's okay. We're all right. It was . . . somebody else."

At school nobody knew anything, and everybody knew everything. Steve Inge had been driving the van, or he hadn't, and nobody knew who owned it. Maybe Boomer Holmberg. Tara Lawrence had been trying to get out, which caused the crash. Or not. They were all either drunk or strung out. Nobody accused them of being sober.

Some people with cars had already driven past the crash site on Lombardy Lane. Word was, the first bouquet of flowers had already been left on the curb where it happened. The six seniors were all in intensive care or being held for observation at Lakeside Hospital, depending on who was talking.

They just barely got us settled down by first period. Then we had speaker-system announcements in all classrooms with the official version. The seniors had been treated for minor injuries and released. Tara Lawrence had lost her life.

We got the announcement in Mr. Atcheson's history class. I knew about half the kids in the room, the

half from Ridpath. We were still getting acquainted
with Mr. Atcheson. He wore patterned sweaters and
corduroy pants and running shoes, but he was a teacher
in spite of the disguise. It really annoyed him that we
didn't know the English had had a Civil War too.

He listened through the PA announcement, tapping
a ballpoint. Then he looked over the class and said,
"First one of the year. What does that mean to you?"

Nobody said anything, but what did it mean? My
mind made a beeline for the driver's license next spring.
And how I didn't want any hysterical talk about how
teenagers aren't responsible enough to drive. Besides,
these people were seniors, apart from Tara. They
weren't us. I sat there, my hands curling around an in-
visible steering wheel, swerving around obstacles, gear-
ing down for sharp turns, thundering through the night.
The room stayed dead silent, waiting Mr. Atcheson
out.

Finally he said, "I hope you'll all be as lucky as you
think you are."

Because of Tara Lawrence's death they didn't play
any PA music between classes that morning. Usually in
those ten-minute intervals through the day we had
multicultural music piped in to keep us in touch with
the outside world: samba-reggae, salsa, gamelan orches-
tra music from Indonesia, rap. I kept an eye out for
Laurel Kellerman.

After last period C.E., Diana, and I all met up in the
math wing. Somehow Diana was ahead of me on the
math track. She was taking geometry, and I was feeling
my way through algebra. C.E. was in a class that would

be called remedial anywhere but Walden Woods. Here it was called "Math for Daily Living."

"Anybody want to go for some yogurt?" he said.

"I want to go over to Lombardy Lane," Diana said. "Let's all go. You too, C.E."

Even this didn't surprise C.E., though he wasn't used to being included in Diana's plans. His eyebrows and his eyelashes are the same color as his face, and this gives him a permanently innocent look. He gazed up at her, agreeable to anything.

"This sounds a little ghoulish for you," I told Diana, though I was willing to check out the crash site.

"Maybe there's a story in it for *The Warrior*," she said.

"Did Garth Lashbrook give you the assignment?"

Me mentioning Garth made Diana's eyelids narrow a bit, like I might be monitoring her phone calls.

"Who waits for an assignment?" she said. "Garth's a good editor. But he'd have to buck every senior on the staff to assign a good story to a tenth grader."

If he's such a good editor, why can't he control his staff? I wondered, but didn't say. We stopped by our lockers, met up again, and headed off to Lombardy Lane.

It's an upmarket neighborhood even for Walden Woods. The lane winds around mature trees through an area of big houses on two-acre lots. We could walk there, and I got a weird feeling down my spine when we were close. A lot of cars were pulled off and parked. When we turned into Lombardy Lane itself, a TV news crew was just pulling away, and the road was full of people walking.

Half the school was there, but we pushed through. They'd taken away the van. But it wasn't hard to figure out. The tread marks slurred across wet ground. Headlight glass frosted the grass. Then the big oak tree was gouged out where the van had hit it square on. The tree would have stopped a Humvee, but the bark was skinned, and the wood behind was splintered and bone-white.

I kept thinking: Tara Lawrence, this girl I'd never said a word to, had been sitting at that library table last night. This girl who'd looked up because an almighty senior had run his hand along the back of her chair. I hadn't even known her, but I wanted her back. Life's got to be more than a TV show where you just get written out of the script. Life's got to have a shape and things you can count on. It was too sudden, too final. Last night she was here. Now we were this crowd of people looking at this damaged tree. I couldn't put any of this together. I couldn't get my mind around it, and I wondered what other people were thinking.

There were four or five bouquets of flowers on the curb now. A girl was laying down a single hothouse rose in a plastic tube. Somebody had put a framed picture of Tara Lawrence on the curb, stood it up like it was on a mantelpiece. Somebody had put down a notebook cover with a lot of names signed on it. Some of the girls were crying, but I couldn't tell if they'd known Tara or not. The place was becoming an instant shrine. We were blocked by the people coming up behind us, and a woman was barging through them.

"It's Mrs. Dalbey from your committee," C.E. said

as she went by us. She looked taller outdoors and a little younger. Her coat was flapping around her, and people got out of her way.

She stopped when she could see the tree. People gave her some space. She looked down at the shrine growing along the curb, then around at us. It was strange. All of us and a teacher, like a field trip.

"Why are you all here?" she said in this ringing voice. "Some of you didn't even know this girl, did you?"

People were turning away from her the way you do when you see a teacher outside school. "I didn't know her either," Mrs. Dalbey said, pointing at Tara's picture. "I only saw her last night, and I didn't know it was the last night of her life."

People were sidestepping Mrs. Dalbey now, shuffling away. "But don't you see?" she said, her voice spiraling up. "Don't you get it? She was any one of you. She could do just as she pleased. She was naive enough to fall in with anybody. And she didn't have sense enough to be let out of the house. She was just like all of you." Then I thought she was going to sob. She was close to sobbing.

"Whoa," somebody said.

But now Mrs. Dalbey turned and started back the way she'd come, shouldering her way through with her head down. I was ready to duck out of her way, hoping she wouldn't recognize me. But—wouldn't you know it? Diana stepped up and put a hand on Mrs. Dalbey's sleeve.

It stopped her. "What?" she said in a tired voice.

"I'm Diana Tobin. I didn't really know Tara either. But I'm sorry. I wish it hadn't happened. It was . . . a waste."

Mrs. Dalbey really looked at her. "It's just so frustrating," she said, like she was talking to another teacher. She started to gesture at the whole scene, but both her hands were trapped in her coat pockets. "We try so hard at that school to . . . get you ready for the world. But you don't want to take the time to get ready. You want it all now. Then you throw yourselves away." Her voice wobbled. "You won't let us save you." Biting her lip, she looked away. "From yourselves."

Here was this teacher burning out before our very eyes. The people around us were pulling back. "Maybe not all of you," she said, and then walked away. The crowd wandered off.

C.E. and Diana and I left too. "How do you do that?" I said to her. "How do you just go up to a teacher who's a stranger?" I couldn't imagine doing that. "Is it because you want to be a journalist?"

"Not really," she said. "I just wanted to know why this one teacher went out of her way to come here and say that to us, even though she knew it wouldn't do any good."

"Why did she?"

"I don't know exactly. But I know she was scared. She wasn't mad. She was scared. Didn't you pick that up in her voice?"

I can't say I did. Scared to me meant something you were while watching a slasher film. Or that moment just before you go to sleep when it occurs to you that something outside might be watching you through the window even though you sleep on the second floor. My idea of scared was probably still back somewhere in grade school.

"You mean she's more scared about death because she's an adult?" C.E. asked Diana.

"Not for herself," Diana said.

"For us?" I asked.

"She may have figured out that we think we can't die," Diana said.

"That could be scary," C.E. said, stroking his chin.

We were strolling now along another street. "But I know," Diana said. "Death was the first thing I ever really learned."

The week went on, and things kept happening, mostly to other people. I looked for Laurel Kellerman down the streaming halls as we boogied between classes to a salsa beat. The school still felt gigantic. Wings ran in every direction. I was still carrying around the printout Mrs. Dalbey had hacked out for me at registration. On a good day I could find my locker on the first try.

Diana decided there wasn't a story in the crash site. It would have to be about Mrs. Dalbey, and she didn't think Garth could get that past the seniors on the newspaper staff. Tara Lawrence was buried on Saturday, and a lot of people didn't like it. They'd wanted a half day off from school for her funeral.

That night I was over at C.E.'s house. It's not a bad piece of property, but really run down. It could use a paint job, two coats. All the lights were on downstairs, and a TV glow came from one upstairs window. They don't lock up. When I strolled in, C.E. was running the vacuum cleaner. An odd sight, because he was wearing his sweatshirt hood up indoors. A troll doing house-work.

"Want to go for a burger?" he said, switching off the Electrolux.

"I just ate."

"Me too."

The Van Meters' living room was mostly furniture with the polish off and no rugs. The only pictures were of C.E.'s dad on golf courses. But they weren't handing the trophy to him. C.E. straightened a stack of *Golf Digest*s and plumped the sofa pillows.

"What's happening over at your house?" he said.

"Nothing." Though it sure wasn't as dead as here.

"So let's go over there," he said.

He called up the stairs to tell his mother where he was going. She was upstairs most of the time, and his dad was almost always out of town.

We smelled fresh popcorn before we got inside our house. C.E. beamed into the kitchen, where Dad was in his apron. A roaster pan was heaped with popcorn, and the syrup simmered on the stove. The plan was for popcorn balls wrapped in orange cellophane for the trick-or-treaters next weekend. It's Dad's annual proj-ect. In a lot of places parents are afraid to let their kids accept homemade treats on Halloween, but nobody was worried about that in Walden Woods.

"Mr. Tobin!" said C.E., this long-lost friend of Dad's. "Good to see you." He marched up and stuck out a hand for Dad to shake.

Just the sight of C.E. never failed to entertain Dad. He wiped a buttery hand down his apron, and they shook hands like a couple of Rotarians. "Can you help me out with some of this popcorn, C.E.?" Dad said. "I've flooded the market. I'm turning into Orville Redenbacher."

C.E. and I took two heaping bowls and a shaker of extra salt into the den. We settled down to watch one of the more recent Dracula films. We had a full house that night. Pace Cunningham had come over to see Diana with Fortnightly Club business to transact. There was going to be a club Christmas dance. Christmas seemed a long way off to me, but if you were a girl and in Fortnightly, you were practically down to the wire.

Having Pace Cunningham over to the house was a bigger deal for Diana than she cared to admit. Pace was a junior. She'd driven over. They were up in Diana's room conspiring, but came down once for some of Dad's popcorn. If anybody could be more organized than Diana, it was Pace. And Pace was gunning to be top boss of Fortnightly. When she and Diana breezed past the den door, C.E. observed them but reserved comment. We were at a crucial point in the Dracula film. Scaly, web-winged creatures with lights in their eyes were working their way up a castle wall.

We pulled the film for the ten-thirty news, to hear how the Warriors had done against the Lake Villa Vikings, on the Vikings' home field. We'd lost, but it was close, and C.E. and I went back to the Dracula.

It was getting late when the phone rang. Deep in his popcorn world, Dad didn't answer it. I picked up in the den, and it was a woman. I waved at C.E. to turn down the sound because the woman was crying. "Who is this?"

It was Mrs. Cunningham. "I can't find my daughter," she said. "I can't find Pace."

"She's here," I said. "She's upstairs with my sister."

A moment of silence then, and Mrs. Cunningham's voice shuddered. "Is she? You tell her to stay right there. I'm coming over."

So we never did see how the Dracula film ended.

"Hey, Pace," I said up the stairs. "Your mom's coming over."

This brought everybody to the front hall, Pace first. Diana was behind her, and Mom in her robe and Marnie in her pajamas. Before Dr. and Mrs. Cunningham got here, Dad was in the front hall, too, in his apron.

They were here fast, bursting in the front door. Mrs. Cunningham went straight across to Pace standing at the bottom of the stairs. She just put her arms around her daughter and held her. "Mother," Pace said in her even tone, not hugging her back, "what is this about?"

Pace's car had been found, flipped, in a drainage

ditch out by the road to the forest preserve. It was empty with the lights still on, and the police had run a make on the plates. Then they'd called the Cunninghams.

"Mother," Pace said, "I have the car keys in my pocket. I've been here since eight o'clock, and I parked right out there on the street."

Which was true, except somebody had hot-wired her Mercury Capri and driven off, right here on Tranquillity Lane.

Pace's parents didn't care about the car now that they knew she was all right. Mrs. Cunningham had another reaction, mainly from relief. She'd stepped back from Pace, or Pace had pulled back. Now Mrs. Cunningham stood there with her hands over her eyes, but the tears came through. Dr. Cunningham put his arms around her.

"Pace could have been kidnapped," she said to Mom. "We didn't know. How could we know?"

Mom wanted them to come in the living room and sit down. Dad said he'd make a pot of coffee. But they kept saying they were sorry to have intruded. They just wanted to get home and take Pace with them.

We watched them go, down the front walk. Pace was saying, "Mother, I can't believe how you're overreacting."

C.E. left next, out the back way to make one final pass at the popcorn.

I started up the stairs. Marnie was perched halfway up in her Garfield bedroom slippers. Mom was still there in the front hall, gazing out one of the narrow windows by the door, though the Cunninghams were gone now. Diana was there too.

"Mom, it's okay," Diana was saying. "Nobody got hurt or anything. It didn't have anything to do with us."

Mom kept staring out into the night, her arms wrapped in front of her. "But when is it our turn?" she said.

Somehow I was too keyed up to get to sleep that night. Again, I reached for the *Fahrenheit 451* book. It was science-fiction or futurist, because that's what Ray Bradbury writes. I flipped it open to read,

> . . . by the end of the day we can't do anything but go to bed or head for a Fun Park to bully people around, break windowpanes in the Window Smasher place or wreck cars in the Car Wrecker place with the big steel ball. Or go out in the cars and race on the streets, trying to see how close you can get to lampposts, playing "chicken."

But I drifted off.

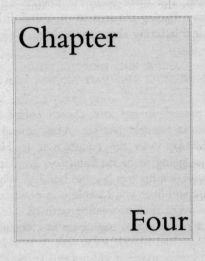

Chapter

Four

Diana sang in our church choir. We'd both been in youth choir, but they'd invited me to lay out a few seasons when my voice changed, and I never got back to them. Boys' voices change. Girls' voices mature. Diana had made the transition into regular choir, alto.

Dad ushers, so he doesn't join the rest of us in the pew until after they've collected the offering. So I'm the man of the family till then, sitting next to Mom and opening Marnie's hymnal to the right page. It's a beau-

tiful church, and there were fall flowers on the altar
that Sunday. During the sermon my mind drifted up to
the gold-leaf lettering about the pulpit:

AND YE SHALL KNOW THE TRUTH,
AND THE TRUTH SHALL MAKE YOU FREE. John 8:32

We passed up the after-church coffee hour and
headed out to Farmers' Market on our annual pumpkin
search. Sunday was the countdown to Halloween,
which was going to be on Saturday. So Dad had the
whole week. It's his top favorite holiday. When Diana
and I were still little and Marnie was practically a tad-
pole, Dad went trick-or-treating with us. Mom would
have to talk him out of suiting up in a costume of his
own. He still had Marnie, of course.

So we were roaming around this stubble field on a
fairly raw day in our church clothes. We wandered all
over Farmers' Market because it's a family tradition and
really makes Dad happy. He and Marnie went up and
down the rows of pumpkins, thumping them. We
drank hot cider with cinnamon and bought gourds,
cornstalks, bittersweet, Indian corn. Dad decorates. You
can even buy autumn leaves in color-coordinated
bunches. We also picked up some leaf bags.

Then it was Monday afternoon, late, and I was
coming back from swim practice. My mind was in free-
fall. I might have been thinking about shaving my legs.
If you were making a total commitment to swim team,
you shaved your body hair and your legs. It was sup-

posed to make you hydrodynamic and faster in the water or something. Actually, it was just for your image. But I had no particular body hair, and I really didn't want to shave my legs. I'd waited a long time for hairy legs.

I came in our front door, aiming at the stairs, and from the corner of my eye I saw Laurel Kellerman in our living room.

She was sitting in the big chair. Marnie was on the floor at her feet, looking up at her. Bells went off in my brain. I'd been turning into the Mad Stalker at school, looking for Laurel all day long, day in and day out, and here she was in our living room.

I shot a glance at the hall mirror. My hair was still swim-team damp. I shrugged out of my backpack, squared my shoulders. Casual, I turned toward the living room and tried to fill up the door.

"Laurel," I said, an octave down. "Good to see you." It sounded like C.E. My voice was betraying me with a C.E. impersonation.

Laurel looked up and smiled, which lit the room.

The whole deal had a perfect logic. Diana and I were on these different schedules. Mom was working longer hours at the shop, so she'd hired Laurel to sit for Marnie every day after school. Fate had delivered Laurel Kellerman to my very door. A home-delivery miracle.

She'd been reading something to Marnie, but put it back in her book bag. Marnie looked up at me and blinked, like she didn't know me in the first moment.

But then, Laurel had been giving her a lot of attention, and I probably hadn't been giving her enough, so I needed to ease in here and not take over.

"I'll get the three of us some cider," I said, stumbling only slightly over my feet. When I brought the cider back, Laurel was talking to Marnie, but stopped.

It was almost evening, and I thought about firelight on Laurel's hair. "Hey, we ought to have a fire." It was already laid in the hearth. All I had to do was touch a match to it. I'd look like that guy in *Hatchet,* the one who could spark flints in dried grass and make fire. Then it was the three of us, Marnie still at Laurel's feet. Me down on the hearth, and the fire catching just right.

It would have been an ideal time to sit there watching the flames, listening to the crackle. But I had to fill up the universe with words. "How come I never see you around school?"

"I'm there," Laurel said, "every day."

"The place is too big," I said. "It's a lonely crowd."

"It is," Laurel said.

"Todd's on the swim team," Marnie said, bless her heart. "And Diana's on the newspaper and in Fortnightly." Marnie kept tabs on us. I suppose we were these complete adults to her. Once in a while I'd catch a glimpse of the way Marnie looked up to Diana and me. Not often. "Todd doesn't do much homework."

"Hey, wait a minute," I said, and Laurel was laughing.

"I do homework," she told Marnie. "I better. This school is harder than my last one."

Marnie thought about that. "But you're really smart, Laurel," she said in her piping voice. "You're a good reader."

And Laurel just reached down and gave her hand a private squeeze.

Then—too soon—Diana came home. She stuck her head into the living room on the way upstairs and said, "Hi, Laurel," like seeing her there was no surprise. I'm the last to know anything.

Laurel was getting ready to go. She was collecting the glasses. "I'll help," I said, scrambling up backward, bouncing off the fire screen. Marnie and I followed her into the kitchen. Laurel rinsed out the glasses, and I watched her hands.

"Your refrigerator's incredible," she said on the way out. "It's full of information." She nodded to all our rosters. "Is it rude to read other people's refrigerators?"

"No," I said. "Absolutely not."

"What does it all mean?"

"Well, we have all these family duties to sign up for."

"Even meals." She must have checked out our lists before, but she was really curious about them.

"Sure. Marnie and I are great cooks," I said, and Marnie agreed. "Don't you cook?" I asked Laurel. I could picture her in a model kitchen pulling together a picture-perfect meal.

"I help my mother," she said.

"Our mom says she could just about manage to do all the cooking, but then we'd take her for granted."

Laurel didn't quite get that. She looked like that wasn't quite right. I tried to picture her family and the house she lived in, but I couldn't. I had her on this other earth in my mind. Now I was trailing her to the front door.

"See you tomorrow," she said to Marnie, winking at her.

Hey, wink at me, I thought. "Let me walk you home."

"No. It's fine. I know the way, and it's still daylight."

"I'd like to."

"Partway," she said, winding a long-tailed scarf around her neck. Her chin nestled in it.

Outside, Dad had arranged cornstalks on the porch. On the door he'd hung this friendly ghost made out of a volleyball in a pillowcase with a face on it. Since one pumpkin was never enough for him, there were six, three on either side of the front steps in graduated sizes, all with carved faces: happy, sad, crooked. Dad had said they were all portraits of us and one extra as Grandma Highsmith.

Laurel looked around at this display. There may have been a nip in the air, because she shivered a little. I couldn't read her eyes. "What's all this mean to you?" she said.

"Dad decorates," I told her, and then we were

scuffing through the leaves in the purple evening haze, and I was going someplace with a girl.

I told her she was great with kids, with Marnie, and she said she had a younger brother in junior high, seventh grade. "It's hard for him moving and changing schools at that age," she said. "You can't even talk to him."

"Bad situation?"

She nodded. "You feel so helpless."

"They get over it," I said maturely. "Diana and I were new here, too, in seventh grade. Did your family come here for the schools?"

"No," Laurel said.

"Then why?"

"My dad was transferred in his job. And then . . ." But she was pulling away from me now like she didn't want any more questions. "Marnie looks up to you and Diana," she said. "I really like kids her age. That's the best age. They're so open. You can tell them things, and they hear."

What I noticed about Laurel was that her eyes weren't as cool as she was. They were warm, and they could flash sometimes. They did when she mentioned her brother, and Marnie. I wanted them to flash when they looked at me, but I didn't know how to make that happen.

"You'll probably be a teacher," I said. I could see her with a class of second graders like Marnie, creating this little world for them.

"I teach Sunday School at church," she said. "Actually, it's not really teaching. I help out in the nursery. About all they learn there is patty-cake and their first hymn."

"What is it?"

"The hymn? 'Jesus Loves Me, This I Know,' " she said.

" 'For the Bible tells me so.' "

Laurel looked up at me then, something astonished in her eyes. " 'Little ones to Him belong.' "

" 'They are weak, but He is strong,' " I said, finishing the stanza.

"But how do you know that?" she said, and suddenly there wasn't anything standing between us. I'd reached Laurel without even knowing. Without having to make any moves.

"It's the first hymn I learned in Sunday School too," I said. But then she stepped up her pace, making a distance between us again. We were in the village center now, going past the Xerox shop. It was all tricked out with black cardboard cats and witches suspended on brooms.

"You better head back," she said.

"You live on Highmeadow, don't you?"

"Yes, but this is far enough."

"Hey, wait a minute," I said. "Is there a national border running down the middle of Walden Woods, and I can't cross it? Is there a limit, or something?"

"Oh, yes," she said, smiling into her scarf. "There are limits." So I turned back then, because she stood very still till I did. But I looked around again to see her walking away, not looking back. And it was like talking to girls and making them interested, making them like you, was this secret code, and everybody knew it but me.

> You could feel the war getting ready in the sky that night. The way the clouds moved aside and came back, and the way the stars looked, a million of them swimming between the clouds . . .

I read in Ray Bradbury's book after I was in bed.

> . . . And the feeling that the sky might fall upon the city and turn it to chalk dust, and the moon go up in red fire; that was how the night felt.

Then the alarm went off in my ear, knocking me into a gray Tuesday morning, and the book was this little paper boat swamped in the sheets on my bed.

Somehow I was running ahead of Diana for once. I charged through breakfast and noticed a message Dad had left on the refrigerator: TROUBLE ON THE FRONT LAWN.

Outside I saw that somebody had torn down his decorations. The volleyball ghost was out on the grass. Somebody had kicked the pumpkins off the steps, and they were scattered around with their sides caved in like they'd been stomped.

I couldn't believe it. This kind of thing doesn't happen on our street. It wasn't that bad, as vandalism goes, but I could picture Dad coming out into the cold dawn and seeing all his careful decorations royally botched up. The pumpkins were beyond repair. That had to have hurt Dad. That got him where he lives.

I'd stuck *Fahrenheit 451* into my backpack, a lucky move. In English class Mrs. Lensky said, "The day of reckoning is at hand." She was holding up the Bradbury book.

We gave her our groan. Hardly six weeks into the year, and we were supposed to have read a book-length book already. And this wasn't English for the Gifted or Language Arts for the Arty—believe me. There were four or five ability levels, and we were somewhere in the middle. But basically we liked Mrs. Lensky, who was a short, reasonable woman who didn't ask us to keep journals.

"Are we going to be tested over this book?" somebody asked.

Mrs. Lensky thought about that. "You might. You never know."

The best-looking girl in class was also turning out to be the star student—Chance MacEnroe. You don't get a lot of girls named Chance around here, but she was a transfer in from Texas. She usually started the class discussion if anybody did.

"I can't even figure out when this story is happening. It's weird, and feels like the future. But they're wearing Walkmen in their ears, and they've got big-screen TV, and those bugging devices. So when is it supposed to be?"

"Check the copyright date," Mrs. Lensky said. Those of us with books did, and it was 1953. So it was historic. Everything we read was.

"So he was writing about the future," Chance said, "and some of it has already actually happened."

"Yes," Mrs. Lensky said. "What's this story about?"

"It's about a time when firemen don't put out fires. They start fires. They've got kerosene in their firehoses instead of water."

"And what are they burning?"

"Books," I said, because I'd read that far. "Whole libraries. I think they've already burned down the libraries. In the story they're going after books that people hide in their houses." The story was too bizarre to believe. So is *Dracula,* but that's different.

"Why do they want to get rid of all the books?" Mrs. Lensky asked. "They go after them all: the Bible, Shakespeare, everything, every word."

"Ideas," I said. "They say the books don't even agree with each other, so they must all be lies."

"Who says that?"

I shrugged. "The government."

"And yet the government isn't really characterized in this novel," she said.

"Society," I said, which seemed safe.

"If they've destroyed the books, what does this society do with its time?"

"Drag racing," I said.

"TV," somebody said. "They've got interactive TV. You can write yourself into it. And they've got these huge screens on all four walls of their rooms."

"Cool," Nick Linstrom said.

"Is this another story about how TV is bad for your brain?" asked bookless Brad Ellerby.

It was and it wasn't.

"What do the people in the novel call TV?" Mrs. Lensky asked.

"That I really didn't understand," somebody said. "They call their television their 'family.' "

"But that's already happening too," Chance said. "Kids in real life now—little kids—come home to empty houses. They turn on TV, and it's still on when they go to sleep. It's like the only family they have."

Mrs. Lensky wanted us to keep the conversation going on our own, the way teachers do. Then Cindy Flagler, who hadn't opened her mouth yet this year, said, "I thought the book was a love story."

We all started to groan at her, but Mrs. Lensky said, "It is."

And it was, at least in the beginning. The fireman in the story, Guy Montag, meets this girl named Clarisse. He's falling in love with her. Then this society wastes Clarisse and her whole family because their thoughts can't be controlled.

"If you had to put the mood of this novel into one word," Mrs. Lensky said, "what would it be?"

"Dumb," said Nick Linstrom, who hadn't read it.

"Fear," Chance said. "I was scared reading it. It's

like a bad dream. It's like people could come into your house and mess with your head."

"And what's the real issue in this book?" Mrs. Lensky said.

"Man's inhumanity to man?" Nick said, taking a stab.

"Try again."

"Man's inhumanity to woman?"

Chance sighed. "It's about thought control. It's about censorship."

"Yes," Mrs. Lensky said. Then she did that thing teachers do—checked the clock to see how much time was left.

So somebody said, "Okay, when's the quiz on this?"

"Do you really want one?" she said. "Do you absolutely insist?"

"No, no," we groaned. "No quiz. We're busy people."

"All right," she said. "After all, you're not in junior high anymore. You ought to be reading for some reason better than passing a test." Her glance grazed Nick. "Or failing it." She seemed to have his number. I'd gone to Ridpath with him, and he never read anything, and he really enjoyed flunking exams. It gave him an image or something.

"We've seen that the book isn't really about the future," she said. "It's a view of the present. The question is, do we have censorship here?"

"You mean like rap lyrics and movie ratings?" somebody said.

"Possibly. But do we have censorship in Walden Woods?"

"I think we're pretty open about things around here," Chance said. "I mean, look." She pointed at the bulletin board with the notice about the AIDS Awareness meeting coming up on Thursday.

We watched Mrs. Lensky while the clock jumped another minute. "How many of you read Anne Frank's book, *The Diary of a Young Girl,* when you were in junior high?"

We all put up our hands. It even rang a distant bell with Brad Ellerby. "It was about the Jewish family who were hidden from the Nazis until they got caught."

"That was the best book we read in junior high," somebody said, "by far."

"You may have been lucky," Mrs. Lensky said.

But we couldn't get her to tell us what she meant. She was doing some kind of number on us, but we didn't know what. She was probably trying to get us to think, but we just wanted her to tell us.

Still another minute to go. Suspense overcame Cindy Flagler. "So if we're not having a quiz over *Fahrenheit 451,* what are we supposed to do?"

"Shut up, Cindy," somebody said.

"You're going to keep your eyes open to see if we have censorship here," Mrs. Lensky said. "And if we do, what forms does it take? You're going to see if the ideas in books are about the real life where you live."

"Projects, right?" somebody said. "Do they have to be written? Does spelling count?"

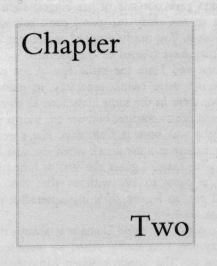

Chapter

Two

The next thing I remember, Diana and I were walking back to school through the October night. "I don't think I've seen her around," she said.

"Who?"

"Who? *Madonna*," Diana said. "Laurel Kellerman, the girl you're thinking about this minute. She's fairly cute, but did you ever overreact. Your eyes got all funny. There were pinwheels where your pupils should be. You were very close to being in a drooling condition."

"Who, me?"

Diana gave out one of her biggest sighs. "Todd, you are so not ready for girls I can't believe it. You nearly lost it. You nearly dropped at her feet."

"I may have tripped on the doormat."

Diana and I are the same age. A lot of people thought we were twins, especially in grade school when we were in the same classroom all day. But we started out life as cousins, because our moms were sisters. Diana was born in California. Her parents were killed out there in a car wreck when she was four. She wasn't with them. I guess she was at home with the sitter. She came to live with us after that, and we adopted her, so legally she's my sister. But it's more than that.

In most of my mind Diana was always there. But in a hazy way I remember when we were four. I was watching out the window when Mom brought her home in a cab from the airport. I remember Diana looking around at us and the house with big eyes, like a little girl in a really sad story.

She wasn't completely a kid, because of this terrible thing that had happened to her. I didn't know what death was, but I knew something really bad had happened. Mom cried when she thought we couldn't hear her, and Mom and Dad both tried to help Diana forget.

But even before kindergarten she was trying to be very independent, like she didn't know if she'd be staying. She'd try to make her own bed in the morning, and she kept all her books and toys in neat piles. Dad sat with her in his lap sometimes, watching TV, but Diana never went to sleep in his arms. She'd sit there very alert, looking around. Maybe she was afraid she'd lose us too.

I remember these things from the early days. It was like Diana never completely unpacked and never really got to be a little kid. Sometimes she was hard to reach. Sometimes she still is. One minute she's Miss Mature. The next, she's detonating like a bomb.

But right from the first she was my sister, and I couldn't picture life before her or without her. And she was Marnie's total big sister. But how much Diana remembered, or how much she thought about who she used to be, I didn't know. She never said.

Through junior high we tried to live on different planets, like any brother and sister. But we were pulling in a little closer to each other to face high school. I'd shot up to five nine in ninth grade, so at least I didn't have to go into high school looking like I was on my knees. Meanwhile, Diana was turning into top-ten-best-looking-girls-at-school. A little tense around the mouth, but big-time beautiful otherwise. Senior guys looked at her, I noticed.

She hit high school running. She didn't go out for everything; she had priorities.

"You have to," she said. One of them wasn't cheerleading. "I'm a human being," Diana said, "not an Energizer Bunny." What she really wanted was to get into Fortnightly Club and onto the staff of *The Warrior,* the school newspaper. By October she'd nailed both.

She was one of the four or five sophomore girls tapped for Fortnightly Club, which at Walden Woods is social heaven. It's a younger version of the clubs Mom belonged to. The members tend to have upscale names like Pace Cunningham and Brinkley Hargrave and Blaine Morrisett.

Also Diana was on *The Warrior* staff before they knew it. Being on the paper was the kind of thing colleges look at, but if you asked me, she had another motive. The editor of *The Warrior* was Garth Lashbrook, senior intellect, debate-team star, and king of the National Honor Society. He was a tall, fairly skinny guy with steel-rimmed glasses who was heading for Harvard. Not everybody's idea of studly, but the kind of guy Diana would be interested in. Though she'd never admit it.

She was already getting phone calls from him. He carried a cellular phone down the halls at school, keeping in touch with his staff or whatever. When he called her at home, a strange, un-Dianaish look came over her, and she'd vanish somewhere with the phone, even into closets. Not cool. But I didn't say anything because I didn't want my head bitten off.

Diana thought that being on the sophomore swim team was one of my better moves. Just having a good time in high school and finding a girl would have been fine with me. In fact just being there was so much better than junior high that I for one didn't even mind being a "grunt," which is what they call sophomores at Walden Woods.

I was still feeling my way, not too sure what to say to girls, trying to figure out what the rules were and who made them. Wondering how everybody but me our front curb. The insurance covered the damage anyway.

They'd upgraded the lunchroom with a salad bar that C.E. and I avoided. The two of us took our trays back, and C.E. was doing his duck walk through the cafeteria chaos. Then he looked down at a girl finishing her lunch at the end of a table. "Hey, Laurel. What it is."

Laurel was sitting there. "Hi, C.E.," she said.

Here's Laurel having lunch by herself two tables over from where C.E. and I have been scarfing down mystery lasagne, mashed potatoes, a full sack of Doritos, and raspberry seltzer. All this time Laurel was there, but I can't see the forest for the trees, or maybe the other way around. The point is, C.E. knows her.

The cat had my tongue. Besides, the bell was ringing, and it was biology. But out in the hall I was practically wringing my hands. "C.E., how do you know Laurel Kellerman?"

"She's in my math class. How do you?"

Laurel was this fantasy I hadn't happened to mention to him. "She baby-sits Marnie. But wait a minute. What do you mean you know her from math class? You mean Math for Daily Living?"

But what was I going to say—that Math for Knuckleheads was about right for C.E., but too dumb for Laurel?

"Yep." He found his locker on the first try and spun the combination. "We're doing fractions or something. She's in my English class too. We're doing *Julius Caesar.*"

"C.E., we did *Julius Caesar* last year at Ridpath."

"We did? I might have been absent that day."

Like we did *Julius Caesar* in a day. Besides, C.E. was never absent, another one of his peculiarities.

I think I could be in love with this girl, I didn't say to him. This is the most incredible girl I've ever met. She's totally unique. She doesn't even pierce her ears. She's cool as college, but she's also like a wounded doe or something. And I have this urge to fly away with her to the moon, or at least to some school-related event in a nondating situation. It could be my hormones, but I think it's love. I didn't say any of this to C.E. He gazed up at me, though, with interest.

We didn't have swim practice that afternoon, but I'd have cut anyway, just to make sure I didn't miss Laurel. I'd forgotten about the pumpkin vandals. When I got home the front lawn was still a disaster area. The volleyball ghost had lost its pillowcase, which had blown around a tree. Still, I went inside first to check on Laurel, and Marnie of course. But they weren't there yet. Marnie stayed at grade school until Laurel could walk her home from there.

I went for some of Dad's leaf bags, and when I got back, they were there at the edge of the yard, hand in hand. Marnie looked really serious, and I thought she was probably upset by somebody trashing the decorations.

"What happened?" Laurel asked.

"Creeps. Early Halloweeners. In the olden days they turned over outhouses." This was for Marnie, because she looked serious enough to cry. She was getting those little dark places under her eyes, and her face looked really pinched.

But Laurel was dealing with her. She bent down till her chin was deep in her scarf and said, "We could do some yard work, couldn't we? We could rake up some of these leaves."

I got more rakes, and the three of us went to work. It was great, and poor old Dad shouldn't have to deal with all this after a hard day at the bank. Besides, I didn't even want him to see this mess. And I had some kind of semifantasy. Here we were raking the lawn, and it was like we were a family. Laurel and I as a mom and dad, Marnie our own kid. And this was our house in some nice, snug future. It was one of my best fantasies.

I felt like piling the leaves up so we could all three jump in. But Marnie was raking seriously, really wanting to get this lawn back in shape. In fact she was working too hard at it. She wore a red yarn cap with a bobbing pom-pom, and her elbows were flying. I wished we could make a bonfire and smell the smoke. I wished Laurel would go to the Homecoming bonfire with me.

We raked until Diana came home, then Mom. I put the cornstalks and bittersweet back around the door but couldn't save the ghost and the pumpkins. We got most of the lawn clean except for the hard-to-get areas under the shrubbery that we left for Dad.

I didn't ask if I could walk Laurel home, partway. I

just fell into step beside her. The raking had put roses in her cheeks, but I had to keep the old conversational ball in play.

"I didn't know you and C.E. had English and math together."

She seemed to see through that, to know I was surprised she was in the easy classes. So I said, "You just seemed more . . . studious than that to me."

"I study," she said, "but school isn't the center of my life."

I didn't know what to make of that. "C.E.'s a character," I said. "We were best friends, more or less, all through junior high. Me and C.E. . . . C.E. and I have probably had lunch every day since seventh grade." Then I added, "We could have lunch."

"You and C.E. and I?" she said.

"Ah . . . you and I."

"Poor C.E.," she said, "out in the cold after all these years."

"He'd understand. I'd hit him till he understood."

"But if we started having lunch together, we'd be an item," Laurel said. "That school isn't particularly friendly, but everybody knows everybody else's business."

We strolled farther. "Being an item would be okay."

"No, it wouldn't," she said, but gently.

There was something pretty final in that, but I decided to keep things light. "Hey, what's wrong with me? I'm on the swim team. Wait a minute. I know. I dress funny, right?" I staggered back and threw out my hands.

She laughed, which is what I'd wanted. "You dress just like everybody else."

Which was true. This far into the semester I knew you wore Dr. Martens on your feet and tied a flannel shirt around your waist. And wore a ballcap backward. It was a sort of top-of-the-line version of a gang-warfare look. I didn't know who made up this dress code, but I was willing to go with it.

And I was willing to walk Laurel all the way home —way willing, but I knew it wasn't in the cards. So maybe another block or two if I could keep us talking.

"I wish we'd gone to junior high together," I said off the top of my head.

"Why?"

Why? Why not? "Because I can't picture you that age." She was put together so perfectly, I couldn't imagine her younger and not quite finished.

"I don't even think about back then," she said, looking ahead. "I don't like to."

"Probably nobody likes remembering junior—"

"No, it isn't that." She shook her head. "I was somebody else completely, and I don't like to remember her."

We went another half block without words. Then I turned back before she told me to. But I watched her walk away into the mysterious evening. The breeze made little swirls of the leaves on the sidewalk between us. And I knew I didn't really know her. But it didn't make any difference.

———

Wednesday was the day C.E. established his reputation
at school, in his Driver's Ed class. I wasn't one of the
many witnesses, because we took it at different times.
But we had the same teacher, Vince Corelli. His first
run out on the test track with Vince Corelli in the passenger's seat, C.E. hits the accelerator on the Dodge
Shadow instead of the brake, mows down six traffic
cones, and slams the concrete divider between the test
track and the athletic field, which is full of PE classes.

This activates both air bags. A lot of people have
never seen this happen. There's C.E. and Vince Corelli
plastered to their seats, their upper bodies embedded in
dual air bags.

"I'll be lucky to get a B in Driver's Ed," C.E. is
heard to say from behind his bag.

Wednesday night was one of our annual family rituals.
Every year on Halloween week Grandma and Grandpa
Highsmith take us to dinner and afterward to the
Kiwanis Club haunted house. This was one of our
childhood customs, but we were still going to the
haunted house for Marnie, and Dad.

Wednesday wasn't a particularly convenient night,
but the dinner was Grandpa Highsmith's treat, and on
Wednesday nights the Rob Roy Restaurant offers two-

for-the-price-of-one dinners for senior citizens. Grandpa keeps a close eye on his money.

One of my earliest memories involves this. Dad and I had been to a hardware store where they'd hung a dollar bill in a frame because this was the first money they'd taken in at this store.

Somehow that stuck in my young mind. Once when we were over at Grandma and Grandpa's, I wandered into his den and started out checking every picture on the wall. Grandpa and Dad came in, and I said I was looking for Grandpa's dollar because Dad said he had the first one he ever made.

Anyway, that Wednesday night Laurel had already gone home, and we were hustling around to get ready to meet Grandma and Grandpa at the restaurant. Dad hadn't changed from work, and Diana and Mom were already downstairs and ready to go. They were dressed in their best. We make this an occasion. I wore my blazer.

Mom called up the stairs for Marnie. "Do you want to wear your witch's costume to show Grandma?" No answer, so Mom went up. When she came back, she said, "I don't know what's the matter. She says she's sick, but she doesn't have a temperature. She doesn't even seem tired. But she really doesn't want to go."

Mom finally decided that Marnie might think she was getting too big for Halloween. Besides, she really liked Laurel and was probably angling to get her to come back for the evening. I could see her point. We had a quick family council, and Mom called Laurel. Dad and I drove over to Highmeadow to pick her up. So at last I was about to see where Laurel lived.

They were next to the Padgetts' in a newer section of the village. It was a low ranch house, and what you could see of the lawn looked very neat. I went up to the door.

Laurel's dad opened it. He was a big guy, thickset, in a flannel shirt. What I really noticed was that Laurel was there too. She was sitting in a chair right next to the front door with her coat on, ready to go. But her dad had opened the door. She hadn't. She didn't even look up in the first moment.

"Mr. Kellerman? I'm Todd Tobin." I'd have put out my hand, but one of his was on the door and the other was on the door frame.

He looked down at Laurel. "I thought you said you were baby-sitting. This looks like a date to me."

Her mother came in from some other room. The first thing I thought of was a bird. A bright little woman, very neat, with an apron. There was a smile on her face, and it was almost Laurel's. She came across the room, hurrying. Then it was all right. "You're Marnie's brother, aren't you? Laurel's ready."

And Laurel was. She stood up, not looking at any of us. But her dad dropped his hand from the door frame, and she eased out.

She took a deep breath when we were in the open air and the door had closed behind us. "I didn't really introduce you to my parents," she said, "but I thought you were probably in a hurry."

"Right. We're running a little late," I said, not even walking close to her in case we were being watched.

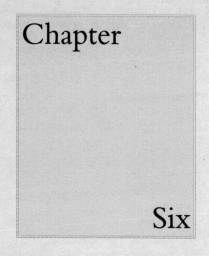

Chapter

Six

The Rob Roy Restaurant is the senior citizens' eatery-of-choice. It's out by Inverness, which is condos around a golf course. On two-for-one night the Rob Roy parking lot was full of sedans: Chryslers, Oldses, Buicks, Caddys. Grandpa Highsmith drove the only used Lincoln in Inverness, though he called it preowned.

The doorman that night was Frankenstein's monster. The lobby was all scarecrows and barrels of apples. Grandpa had on his plaid pants. Grandma was looking at her watch. When she spotted us, she said,

"Where in the world is Marnie? Is it that bug that's going around?" Grandpa Highsmith got me in a hammerlock, though now he had to stand on his toes, but it's his traditional greeting for me.

They were holding a table for us, and we had the surf-and-turf, another tradition. "You're looking tired and drawn," Grandma said to Mom, who was looking her best. She didn't even look old enough to be our mother, if you asked me. "You're burning the candle at both ends. I don't know why you're knocking yourself out at that resale place."

"We do good work," Mom said in a tight voice she never used with us. "We're just about supporting a day-care center with our profits."

"Well, I'm sure it's a worthy cause," Grandma said, "but what kind of people shop in a place like that, anyway?"

"You'd be surprised," Mom said. "We have some nice things. We get a lot of customers coming over from Inverness."

"Buying clothes that other people have worn?" Grandma's eyes got big behind her bifocals.

"Do you have a men's department?" Grandpa asked, always alert to a bargain. He'd been talking Dad through the sand trap on the seventh fairway of Inverness golf course, and Dad's never had a two-iron in his hands. "I could use some ties, couldn't I, Alice?" But you never know when Grandpa's kidding. He peered up at Grandma, who was bigger than he was.

Maybe it was his way of cooling Grandma and Mom down. Mom was always on her guard around

Grandma—probably something left over from their past. Once in a while I caught a glimpse of what Mom had been like as a young girl, and usually it was when Grandma was around. Mom liked to keep pretty cool, but she had her limits, kind of like Diana.

I drifted in and out of the conversation. Most of me was back at Laurel's house, watching that front door open and seeing her dad there. The more I thought about it, the bigger he got. I wondered if I could have handled the situation any better.

Maybe Laurel was this princess in a tower, and her dad was this ogre. I could put on my armor and go look for a white horse. But real life tended to be more complicated than that. Anyway, maybe it wasn't that she didn't like me. Maybe she was afraid to like anybody.

Then Grandma gave Mom a break and turned her guns on Diana and me. "I read in *The Suburbanite* about that girl at your school who was killed in that awful wreck. It just made my heart stop."

And Diana, not like a kid at all, reached out and put her hand over Grandma's. "I know, Grandma. It was terrible." Diana's incredible.

Nothing slows down Grandma, though. "I'm just so relieved that you two children aren't old enough to drive. When you are, I can tell you I won't have a single night's sleep. What do you need to drive for, anyway? You can walk to school."

Now Mom had her hand over her mouth, and seemed to be grinning.

"Dessert's included," Grandpa said, so we moved

on to a choice of mince pie or something called pumpkin whip. We were still on for the Kiwanis Club haunted house even without Marnie. Both Grandma and Grandpa figured that Diana and I wanted to go. I often wondered just how old they thought we were. Dad was totally psyched for it. We went in two cars.

Fright Night at Hangman's House is basically the same deal every Halloween. But this year they'd outdone themselves. It's a real farmhouse, and they had a gas jet shooting flames out of the roof into the night sky. Fog rolled out from under the foundation. The parking lot was full, and the crowd-control people waved cars in. A fire-breathing dragon was wandering around.

Even on a school night there was a line to get in. We had to wait long enough to check the people coming out. Only one very small kid was crying, and everybody else was cool. "Not a good sign," Dad said.

To keep us entertained they piped out organ music playing new-age funeral dirges. Along the path were signs like

DON'T THINK OF IT AS BEING EATEN ALIVE
THINK OF IT AS ACUPUNCTURE WITH BIG NEEDLES.

Then we were up on the porch edging toward the door, which is probably the best part, when you have a real urge to run the other way. Last year I tried to be too old for the whole experience. This year I decided to go with it. Then we were next. A black velvet curtain parted, and a personality in a shroud, fright wig, and black-and-white makeup, who said she was "Fannie Fear, Queen of the Eternal Night," welcomed us to Thirteen Rooms of Doom.

As a party of six we were issued a rope to hold on to and keep us together. Grandma herself gets into this. She'd changed into sneakers.

The first part was blacked out, with unnamed things that brushed your head. Dad was at the front of the rope. Diana was behind him to keep him steady. I was between Mom and Grandma, who had me in a death grip, saying into my ear, "I can't see my hand in front of my face. It's dark as a pocket in this place. Todd, you catch me if I start to fall." Like I'd know until she hit me with her full weight. Grandpa brought up the rear.

One room we came to was a space station lost in space. A reactor-coolant leak had set off a smoky haze, and there were out-of-work actors as aliens, coming at you.

We went through Freddy's Revenge and along the Hall of Grave Secrets with body parts and bats, then up a stairway called Jason's Journey. The rooms upstairs weren't bad. You just got a quick look into Lizzie Borden's Bedroom, and there was somebody in a big wig and a long dress, chopping up her parents.

"That woman was enormous," Grandma said in my ear, but I personally thought it was a guy. Come to think of it, so was Fannie Fear. Then there was Chainsaw Chamber, which gave everybody a buzz.

After that we were in the Ancient Egypt area, approaching the Mummy's Curse, and of course Dad's our front man. Just ahead was an open mummy case. The mummy was inside, with black light on it and a lot of oozing green mummy wrappings. Pretty hokey, but Dad was checking it out. Then the mummy's hand lunged out for Dad's throat.

He yelled and jumped back, lighting on Diana. We were all yelling now, fumbling the rope. Mom was backpedaling onto my feet. Grandma's swinging purse slammed the side of my head.

And Dad was saying to the mummy, "That was *great*. I want to shake your hand." But the mummy was back in his case by then, playing dead.

We got through it, and nobody's hair turned white overnight. We get through it every year, and Grandpa seems to think it's worth the price of admission. Out in the parking lot Dad said, "They're getting the bugs out of it, so to speak. I give this year's effort my three-cleaver award."

On the drive back to Walden Woods we were on the expressway for two exits and off onto Tamarack Road. I was up front with Dad, and we could see the flashers on the cop cars ahead. Closer, a wrecker flashing yellow was pulled up from the other direction, and a paramedic van.

You could see how it had happened. We were only about the fifth car in the backup. A Toyota Camry had jumped a curb and hit a concrete light post. Took the front end out of the car, and it had bounced back to block the street. There was a certain amount of chrome stripping scattered around. Uniformed people were all over the place. Dad and I got out.

There was blood on the dashboard. "Somebody got a banged head out of this," a cop was saying. The top of the steering wheel was bent. Somebody had made a quick exit, because the keys were still in the ignition.

"Fits the profile," the cop said. "Kids. Joyriders. Two of them, it looks like." Both front doors on the Camry were open. "They might not have been big enough to see over the hood. But they meant to wreck it." The Camry had local tags, and we hung around till the cops found the registration in the glove box and read it out, but it didn't belong to anybody we knew.

They cleared a lane around the car. We could go on, though they let the oncoming cars go first. "I'm glad Grandma didn't see that," Diana said.

At home Laurel's dad wasn't parked out front, waiting for her. She met us at the kitchen door with her coat on and her book bag on her shoulder. "Marnie's asleep," she said, something rushed in her voice. I couldn't see her eyes. "My dad can't come to pick me up. They had to take my little brother to the hospital. I just got the call. He's hurt. Actually he's sick. Mr. Tobin, can you take me there?"

I went, too, though I didn't know if Laurel wanted me along. She sat up front with Dad, and I went in the back. Lakeside Hospital was a fifteen-minute drive at that time of night.

"I'm sure it's going to be all right," Dad said to her,

and he wasn't the same guy he'd been all evening at the Hangman's House. He was right there for her.

When we'd pulled up at the emergency-room entrance at Lakeside, Laurel's hand was already fumbling with the car door. "Don't—"

"We're coming in with you, Laurel," Dad said. "I want to know how your brother is." So she had to let us walk her inside.

Mrs. Kellerman was sitting on one of the slick plastic benches in the waiting area. She stood up when she saw Laurel, but they didn't rush into each other's arms or anything. She was dressed the way she'd been at home, with a coat neatly folded over her arm.

"Mother, what—"

"It's going to be all right, Laurel. It's not in our hands." She looked up at Dad. "You're Mr. Tobin. We hear so many nice things about you from our neighbors, and from Laurel. It's very good of you to bring her." Then her quick gaze shifted because Mr. Kellerman came out of the door. Even in here he was massive.

Overlooking me, he put out his hand to shake Dad's. "They've got things under control now. It's not major. Appreciate your help.")."

"If there's anything else we can do . . ."

"No, no," Mr. Kellerman said. "We're going to bring Billy home tonight."

We left then. Laurel didn't look at me, or anybody. She was pulled way back inside herself, staring away at nothing. Dad let me drive, and I just happened to have my learner's permit with me. I was never without it. I slept with it in case I had a driving dream. As I crept cautiously out of the parking lot, Dad said, "Well, which was it? Was the boy injured or was he sick? Funny family."

I didn't say anything. Laurel hadn't wanted me near her house. It was like her dad didn't trust her. And now this with her brother, whatever it was. I couldn't add it up.

Then Dad said, "What do you suppose goes on inside all these houses that we never know about?" He was hunched over like he has to be in the car, gazing out his window. We were driving along a typical Walden Woods row of houses—warm light beaming out of the windows and making long shapes on the lawns. "Are we lucky and don't know it?"

"Who?"

"Us," Dad said. "Our family."

"Maybe we are."

From the corner of my eye I noticed somebody trudging along the dark sidewalk. Hood up, hands bunched in his sweatshirt front, duck walk. It could only be C.E.

Using the turn signal, I edged over to the curb. He didn't seem particularly surprised to see us. Like Dad and I make regular patrols of the streets every night. I know C.E.'s a wanderer, but when he came over to the car, I said, "What are you doing on Hospital Drive at this time of night?"

"Walking off supper," he said. "You guys want to stop by Long John Silver's for some fishwiches? How's it going, Mr. Tobin?" He and Dad shook hands.

Dad slid over, and C.E. piled in, and we headed off to Mill Lane to take him home. When we got there, every light was on downstairs at their house, and the front door was standing open.

"C.E.," Dad said, "you folks ought to be more careful about locking up your house. Is your mother at home?"

"As a matter of fact, she isn't, Mr. Tobin," C.E. said. "I just didn't think too much about it when I left."

He got out and gave us a wave, but Dad told me to wait till he was in the house. We watched C.E. walk across the unraked yard and up the steps. In a way it was funny. This pointy-headed shape of a guy. In a way it wasn't.

Then he was inside, shutting the door, turning off the porch light. And Dad said, "Yes, we're lucky."

Our house was quiet when we got back. We climbed the stairs, and Diana looked out of her door, wanting to know what had happened.

"Apparently nothing too serious," Dad told her. "They're taking Laurel's brother home tonight. They didn't seem to want to talk about it."

Then I was asleep. Then I was awake, and time had passed. I can sleep through tornadoes and missile attacks. But some sound woke me. I lay there about half aware, hearing something like water. It wasn't outside. The ivy made a dry sound against the house. Now I had to go to the bathroom.

Mom and Dad's room has its own bathroom. The other one opens onto the hall. I stumbled across, not even seeing a line of light under the door. When I went in, I was blinded by white light bouncing off the tile walls, and my feet were slapping in cold water all over the bathroom floor.

Marnie was there. I couldn't get a fix on her at first. She was over by the toilet, and her pajamas were sopping wet. Her mouth opened when she saw me, but she held back the sound. I couldn't think what was going on here.

There was stuff all over the floor, black stuff beginning to float. She was trying to pull something out of the toilet, also black. It was like a bad dream. "Marnie—what?"

"I—the toilet got all clogged up, and I can't fix it." We were both whispering, and she was just on the edge of crying.

I sloshed across the floor over the black shapes, and it felt like walking on ground glass. "What is this stuff?" But the water was running over the toilet rim, and Marnie was still trying to drag out this big sopping black rag. "It's like it won't let go," she said, gasping and sobbing.

So I took it out of her hands. They were shaking and blue with cold. I had to get my whole arm down in the toilet. And I worked my hand around down there until I could get the material loose. When it came out, I nearly fell backward onto the flooded floor. The water drained then, and the toilet made one last hiccup sound. It looked like the tide was going out.

I was holding this slimy piece of black cloth that glittered with little sequins and beads hanging from wet threads.

"Marnie, what is this?"

But I knew. It was her witch's costume. She'd cut it up. She'd taken a pair of scissors to it and tried to flush it down the toilet. I wanted to yell at her. But she was just standing there in her sopping pajamas, her eyes full of tears and her shoulders sagging. I should have just grabbed her and held her for a minute. I was down on one waterlogged knee. We were both wringing wet.

"You shouldn't put things down the toilet," I said, whispering. "They won't . . . fit."

But she wasn't looking at me. She was turned away, facing the blank wall.

"We better get this cleaned up, okay?"

Still she wouldn't look my way. Now she was embarrased, on top of whatever else she was feeling. It would have been better if she'd been crying. "Come on, let's get some of these towels and see what we can do."

"We can't use the good towels. Mom—"

"They can go in the washing machine tomorrow. And Mom will have to know. She's going to wonder where your witch's costume went, right?"

We went to work with the bathroom sponge and the good towels and threw the glittery rags of the witch's costume into the bathtub. I don't know how long we worked, wringing the towels out in the tub. I saved a couple back to dry ourselves. Marnie was so tired, she was staggering.

"You go on to bed now. Take a towel and put on dry pajamas. Can you manage that?"

She nodded, her chin down. Then she was walking away, barefoot across the smeary floor.

"Marnie, why did you do it?" I whispered.

She turned at the door and looked back almost at me. "It was bad," she said. "It was a bad costume. It was—" and without any sound her mouth shaped the word: "*evil.*"

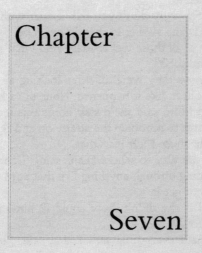

Chapter

Seven

Behind my eyelids I could feel morning coming. Then I was up, swaying, my whole body screaming for more sleep. Dad was down in the kitchen. The sight of me this early nearly made him spit coffee into the sink. Then Mom came in.

"Maybe you better let Marnie stay home from school this morning and sleep," I said. "She was up in the night."

"Then she really was sick," Mom said. "Why didn't you call us?"

"She wasn't sick."

"Then—"

"Mom, why don't you talk it over with Marnie?"

But Diana swung in then in her robe. "What's the meaning of all those wet towels? And what's that mess in the bathtub?"

So now they were all three looking at me. I told them about it, like it happened. None of us knew what it meant. Mom said she'd stay home this morning and take Marnie to school in the afternoon and skip a day at the resale shop. I left it at that.

On the way to school Diana said, "I don't remember us going through anything like that at Marnie's age. I just don't get it."

And if she didn't, how could I? But I said, "You went through a lot."

"I held everything in," Diana said, "but Marnie kind of goes to pieces over things. Remember her in kindergarten?"

I'd about forgotten that. Marnie hadn't gone to play school, so kindergarten came as a real shock to her. It scared her—being away from home and around a bunch of rowdy kids. She kind of reverted—hid when it was time to leave the house and started sucking her thumb again. But Mom talked her into it somehow and afterward she was fine.

In Atcheson's World History, I was half in the bag, just barely there. Toward the end of class I surfaced to hear him saying something about the AIDS Awareness meeting after school in Mrs. Noyes's library. The morning crept, but I managed to be up for Driver's Ed.

The lunch-hour rumor involved Steve Inge. Word was that he must have been the driver of the Tara Lawrence death van because his parents had pulled him out and sent him away to boarding school.

I still felt like Dracula in daylight. Being this tired made me start free-associating or whatever. I can't say I was really waking up the way Mrs. Lensky meant. But I began to put a couple of things together; a couple—not more.

"C.E., is Laurel in school today?" I said to him as he was tucking into a brace of burritos.

"She was in English," he said. "You know, *Julius Caesar* isn't too bad. Shakespeare got all these famous quotations together and made a play out of them."

I was on my feet by then. In fact I was standing on my chair, scanning the lunchroom. I saw her across the room. Above the unbelievable roar I noticed how alone she was there at the end of a table. She wore just this dark blue turtleneck and a gold chain, and everything about her was exactly right. I wondered why everybody in the cafeteria didn't notice her, every guy. I dropped down and went in her direction.

Hooking a spare chair, I moved in beside her. She looked up and gave me her all-purpose smile.

"How's your brother? How's Billy?"

"Fine," she said. "He'll be out of school a few days. He won't mind that."

She was folding up a plastic sandwich bag, neatly with her mother's hands. She never had much small talk, and she could have used some now, because I took a flyer and said, "How bad was he hurt?" I didn't really know this. I didn't really know anything.

"Hurt?" she said, and her eyes looked trapped. "He wasn't hurt. He got sick."

"Was it concussion? A head injury?"

"You went back to the hospital," she said in a different voice. "You checked the records or something." Her hands were still among the things on her tray.

"No, I didn't. I don't think they show records."

"He broke his nose," she said.

"He hit it on the steering wheel."

She looked away, checking the room, then back at me. "How do you know that?"

"I don't, but we saw the wreck. Then half an hour later we were taking you to the Lakeside emergency room. It was Billy, wasn't it? He's the phantom joyrider and demolition expert, him and a buddy." I wasn't trying to hurt her, or scare her. She was just so closed in on herself that I wanted to let her out.

"He can find the wrong people every time," she said. "He didn't say who the other boy was, but of course with Billy it's always somebody else's fault. Usually it's somebody a little older. But even then Billy's the leader." She sighed, just a regular big-sister sigh. "And it's always his first time."

"But it wasn't his first time, was it? He stole Pace Cunningham's Capri, didn't he? And flipped it?"

"He got hurt that time too," Laurel said, barely aloud. "But Mother could patch him up."

"Your parents know what he's up to?"

"Nothing very . . . subtle about Billy," she said.

"He acts everything out. When he was little, it was just tantrums. Now it's more than that. He wants them to know what he's up to. He likes seeing them covering up for him. Last night my dad told the emergency-room people that Billy had fallen off his bike and hit his nose."

"I'd think your dad would tear his head off and chain him up against the basement wall . . . if you don't mind me saying so."

"But Billy's a boy," Laurel said, giving me the first really direct look ever. "Billy can do no wrong."

The bell rang, and she stood up, wanting to turn away from me. "You won't tell anybody, will you?"

"It'll be our secret." I wanted something between us, even this. She vanished into the crowd. She was good at that.

I walked partway to biology with C.E. Something else was nagging at me now, something about C.E.'s late-night stroll. "Were you at the hospital last night, C.E.?"

"Who says I was?"

"Nobody. But I was just thinking. Laurel and her family were in the emergency room, and you were sort of at large in the general area."

C.E. trained two pale eyes up at me. "Nope, I wasn't in the emergency room." Then the crowds swallowed him too. C.E.'s eyes are very innocent, but they're also very close together.

After school on my way to swim practice, I was heading down the hall past the library. Diana was there with a notebook in her hand, and she was buttonholing

Pace Cunningham by her locker. "Pace, are you coming to the AIDS Awareness meeting?" Diana said.

Cool Pace would have brushed by, except Diana was in Fortnightly. She hesitated. "Are you in charge of it?" Pace was definitely a political animal. She'd go to your meeting if you'd go to hers.

"No," Diana said. "I just think it's important."

"Why?" Pace said. "Actually, I've got a yearbook meeting, and I'm running late." She gave her watch a busy-woman glance and moved on.

The after-school crowd had thinned, and Diana spotted me. I, too, was ready with my excuse, but she said, "I'm going to write something on the meeting for *The Warrior*. And, no, Garth didn't assign me the story. I have a feeling he didn't assign it to anybody."

Now Mrs. Noyes was propping open the library doors. An AIDS poster hung on each of them. She recognized me and said, "Sophomore, right?"

"This is my sister," I said, hoping to ease out of this. "She's going to do an article on your meeting."

"Great," Mrs. Noyes said. She was scanning the hall. This whole end of school had emptied out, except for a few teachers coming to the meeting. "We'll need all the publicity we can get," she said to Diana. "What year are you?"

"Sophomore," Diana said.

"Oh, are you two twins?" But now Mrs. Noyes turned to greet Mr. Atcheson and Mrs. Lensky, who'd arrived for the meeting.

"I know," Diana said to me, "you've got swim

practice, and Coach Hopkins is on your case. But at least come in for a minute and meet the speakers."

Enough chairs were set up in there for an audience of a hundred, easy. Except for a handful of teachers, nobody had turned up.

Diana was already working the row of four speakers who sat facing this emptiness. Maybe she was trying to show them at least a couple of students, and maybe she was stalling. There was even a microphone on the podium, which was beginning to look pathetic. The meeting should have started ten minutes ago. I met the speakers but didn't catch their names. One was a doctor. One was a woman.

This didn't take up much time, and Mrs. Noyes was getting desperate. "Look," I muttered to Diana, "I've really got to—"

"I'll walk you out," she said. Mrs. Noyes was over at the library doors now, checking to see if by any chance her audience was dawdling around out in the hall.

I was hoping to slip past her without being missed when we all noticed two guys and a girl up on the stairway landing. They were looking down to monitor the library doors. One of them was Boomer Holmberg, all two hundred and forty pounds of him. He was wearing Umbro soccer shorts this late in the season, either because even cold can't touch him, or to show off his massively muscled legs.

Mrs. Noyes said, "Well, are you three up there coming to the meeting?"

"No way," Boomer said. The guy with him snorted. The girl dipped behind Boomer's shoulder and giggled.

"Then why are you hanging around up there?" Mrs. Noyes asked.

"Just checking out who's coming to your meeting," Boomer said, his voice echoing in the stairwell. "We want to see who the faggots are."

I left then, heading for the gym.

Coach Hopkins could take me or leave me. About the only time he noticed me was when I was swimming diagonally across all six lanes or when I was late, like today. Then I got a blast from the whistle. The best part for me was just being in the pool itself, trying to be in charge of my own breathing and pulling through the water. Not seeing much through the goggles, not hearing much but my own heartbeat and the static behind my earplugs. Sometimes being in this other watery world helped me think.

He put us through it: three flys—forty-five repeats. We usually stayed on longer, horsing around in the water, getting our strength back. I was about to swim a couple laps more just to see if I could straighten out my stroke. My toes curled around the tile edge of the pool. Then it came to me.

Another puzzle part fell into place, or seemed to.

I headed to the locker room. I didn't bother to shower, so I went home smelling like chlorine.

Mom was at the kitchen table when I came in. She was dressed up and looking good. She could do commercials. But it was like she'd been sitting there doing nothing, which wasn't like her. I got close enough for her to give me a hug around the waist. "You reek," she said.

I asked her where Marnie was.

"She's upstairs with Laurel. I wanted Laurel here today even though I was home. I thought it might help. Marnie slept till eleven. But I couldn't get anything out of her, and she wanted to go to school."

"Was she embarrassed about ruining her costume or something?"

"Something," Mom said. "I asked Miss Rosen if I could sit at the back of the classroom. I thought maybe I hadn't been giving Marnie enough attention. You know how busy we get. But all afternoon she sat staring straight ahead. Maybe she'll be better with Laurel. . . ." Mom's voice trailed off.

"I'd like to try talking to her," I said, which surprised Mom a little. We went up to Marnie's room. Laurel was there, and they were coloring. Marnie was. She had her crayons out, working away, and seemed cool. The two of them sat together on the foot of the bed.

Laurel looked up suddenly, but then she smiled and nodded at us over Marnie's head. Marnie looked up and said, "I'm coloring. Laurel brought me a coloring book." I'd thought she was probably outgrowing coloring books, but Laurel had brought it so it was special.

The room was like Toys "R" Us. Every stuffed animal, her Barney dinosaur, dolls of every size. Sometimes Mom tried to talk her into paring down her collection. Marnie agreed on principle, but couldn't ever give up any particular one. "That's a keeper," she'd say, even about a bald Barbie doll.

"Marnie."

"I'm not going to talk about last night, Todd." She never looked up from her coloring. "No way." She was giving it a hundred and ten percent of her concentration, but she was ready for me.

"No. Right," I said. "I mean the other night when you had a bad dream or whatever. And Mom came into your room?"

"I don't remember that."

Beside me Mom made a little sound.

"Marnie, yesterday you didn't want to go out to dinner with us and Grandma and Grandpa. You didn't want to go to the haunted house."

"It was cool," she said, sounding like me. "Laurel was here."

Laurel listened.

Then I went for the big one. "Do you know who knocked all the pumpkins off our front steps and tore down the ghost?"

Marnie's crayon skidded. "Creeps," she said. "Early Halloweeners."

I waited maybe a whole minute. Then, as quiet as I could, I said, "Marnie, you did that."

The coloring book slid off her knees and hit the floor. Mom started forward, but the look on Marnie's face stopped her. She looked older, like someone else. Her jaw was clenched. Crazily, I thought of all the mismatched teeth inside clenched together too.

I could even picture it. Marnie getting up in the dark and coming down through the house in her pajamas. Going outside and throwing the pumpkins all over the yard, jerking down Dad's volleyball ghost. I could see her doing this in the dark while the rest of us were asleep, and then climbing back up the stairs afterward with the pumpkin seeds stuck to her feet.

"Marnie, is it Halloween? Is Halloween bad?"

Without her coloring book, her hands didn't have anything to do. She swung her heels against the bedspread. I thought she was stonewalling us, but then she said, "There are witches."

"Is that why you didn't want to wear your witch's costume?"

She nodded, and her eyes were dry and sure. "There are real witches. Black is their color."

Next to me Mom was tensing up.

"There might be people who think they're witches," I said. "Hey, there are people who think they're Elvis Presley."

Marnie shook her head. "No, there are witches. Some of them look just like everyday people. Halloween is their special night. They kidnap children and kill them. More children disappear on Halloween night than any other night of the year."

The room was dead silent.

"There are real witches. They do the devil's work."

"Marnie, wait. The devil? You mean the guy with the red tail and the pitchfork?"

Something went through her, and she looked at me like I'd said words I couldn't ever take back. I'd never seen her so scared.

"If you don't know the power of the devil," she said, "you go to hell. You burn for a long time, for eternity. Anybody who doesn't believe that burns in hell." Then at last Marnie looked up straight into Mom's eyes.

"Who told you these things, Marnie?" Mom said.

"Laurel told me."

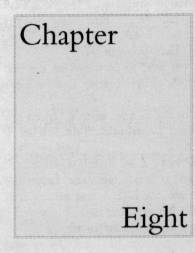

Chapter

Eight

It was almost dark out, and there was only one light on in Marnie's room, the little lamp on her dresser. Laurel's face was shadowed.

"Marnie," Mom said, "Laurel didn't tell you those things, did she?"

Marnie nodded, but wouldn't look up. Her hand was creeping back to touch Laurel's. Laurel was totally quiet, and calm. "Laurel told me."

"Didn't you hear it from kids in the playground or someplace?" Mom asked. "Kids trying to scare you?"

"No," Marnie whispered. "They don't even know. They think Halloween's fun. They don't know. A teacher could be a witch. You can tell if they read you ghost stories. Then you can tell."

Mom went over to sit down on the bed. Marnie hunched her shoulders, bracing against a hug. Laurel stood up.

"I'll get to the bottom of this," Mom said to us.

"You have," Laurel said. "I did tell her. It all happens to be true."

I couldn't have heard that. It was like I still had my earplugs in and was hearing static. Laurel moved past me and out into the hall. It was getting late, and her dad didn't like her out after dark. I followed her down the stairs, and my feet were numb.

Laurel reached for her coat. Mom was coming down behind us, leaving Marnie up in her room. From the stairs she said, "Who are you, Laurel?"

She looped the scarf over her head. "I'm a believing Christian." But she didn't look at Mom or me, and I was right there beside her.

"Surely not," Mom said.

Laurel's eyes flashed. Her face was composed, but not her eyes.

"A believing Christian would never try to frighten a child. Marnie's a little girl, and the rest of us in this family are all grown-ups in her eyes. We forget how young she is, and vulnerable. She was so eager for the attention you gave her, Laurel. And you used that."

"I was trying to save her," Laurel said, pulling on

her coat. "You people can't save her. You people are lost yourselves."

Mom turned on the stairs and started back up. "Wait here a minute."

I thought Laurel might leave anyway. But she turned to the mirror that hung in the hall and just touched her hair. It was such an ordinary thing to do, just an everyday thing.

"Laurel, there's been some kind of a mix-up. Marnie's got it wrong or heard it wrong. You didn't tell her all that spook-show stuff is real."

She turned to me, and it was Laurel except without the careful smile. "Satan is everywhere, and his followers are here. In grade school it's all those hideous Halloween decorations that make little children love evil. That's what turns them into the kind of people you and I go to school with every day. Don't you know the devil and his workers are in that high school? Are you that blind? You wonder why I'm in the easiest classes I can find. I'll tell you why. The lessons they teach in school are all meant to kill God in your heart. The teachers are all atheists, whether they know it or not. I have to go to school, but I don't have to lose my soul."

Mom was coming back down the stairs with her purse, holding out money. "Here, this is what we owe you." Now it was like I wasn't even there. It was just Laurel and Mom, and Mom's face was like a mask.

"I suppose you don't want me back."

"No. Later, I may feel sorry for you. Now I just want you out of my house."

Laurel left, and I was staring at the door that had closed behind her. In my head it was some other day. And I was walking Laurel partway home, scuffing through the leaves, making the time last.

When I turned around, Mom was saying, "What should I have done? I've never ordered anybody out of the house in my life. But what Laurel told Marnie wasn't sane."

I wanted to defend Laurel, but I didn't know who she was.

"All I know is that she came into our house and hurt my child," Mom said, "and we let her in."

It couldn't have been the Laurel in my mind, though. I wanted to go after her, start running down the streets. I made a move toward the door, and Mom said, "No, Todd. Let her go. I need you here. How many times was Laurel here with Marnie? I can't even remember."

"Not that often," I said. "Just a few times. I don't see how . . . anything could have happened." But I thought about Laurel and Marnie together after school. The conversations that had stopped when I came in. The pamphlets Laurel had slipped back into her book bag. That time Marnie had looked up at me like I was a stranger.

"It doesn't take these people long," Mom said. "You read about people like this, people who are pro- grammed—brainwashed. I thought they lived some- where else." Her voice cracked then. "I didn't know they came into your house."

Now from the back of the house we heard Dad. He came up the hall with something in his hand. But everything was like a dream now with half-familiar people doing almost normal things.

"Last one for rent in the shop," he said, holding up the tape of a movie. "We ought to buy our own copy."

It was *The Wizard of Oz*. Dad rents it every year, and we sit around eating popcorn and saying the lines before the characters do because we know that movie cold. It's the Judy Garland favorite with Margaret Hamilton as the wicked witch.

Mom and Dad went into the den to talk. I stood out in the hall, trying to decide what to do. Then I went upstairs. Marnie's door wasn't quite closed.

I could see in there that her closet door was shut tight as usual. A long time ago she decided that something really scary lived in that closet. Then one night the closet door popped open by itself and sort of swung out into the room. Marnie didn't even scream. Mom found her the next morning asleep under her bed, all wound up in her comforter. "She could have suffocated," Mom said.

We all tried to talk her out of it. I myself went in that closet, stumbling around on her little shoes, saying, "It's great in here. This is a good closet. And totally empty."

But Marnie wasn't buying any of this. Finally Diana said, "If she's so sure there's a monster in the closet, let's make it a good one for her." So we talked about this nice beastie in there with plush fur like a toy and no teeth.

Marnie saw right through that. I don't think she ever forgot her monster in the closet. I think she just learned to live with it.

I knocked on Marnie's door. A long pause and then from inside: "What?"

"Marnie, we're down for dinner tonight. You and me."

"No, we're not," came a faint voice. "It's Dad and Diana's night."

I stuck my head in. I was hoping she'd be coloring or doing something. She was on her bed, facing the other way with her knees pulled up. It was a small bed, but she looked lost in it.

"Dad's . . . busy," I said, "and Diana's not home yet. She's late or something."

I wanted Marnie to roll over and look at me, but she didn't. "So let's take charge of dinner."

"Can't," she said. "I have to do my Jell-O the night before."

"We'll go with a green salad. Then we'll make Dad and Diana cook when it's our turn. That'll be fair."

I waited. She was in these small jeans and a miniature sweatshirt with cut-off sleeves that showed her knobby shoulder. Her hair made a fuzzy halo in her pillow. I figured I'd leave, and maybe she'd follow.

Down in the kitchen I was at the counter, reaching for an onion and my goggles, when she came in. She hung around at the door, and I didn't know whether to look over at her or keep working.

"Want to see me juggle up to three cans of pork and beans?"

"Seen it," she said. She was cautious, watching me. "Don't say anything bad about Laurel."

"Who, me?" I was cool, but the goggles hung in my hand. "I like Laurel," I said, feeling my way. I could sense the suspicion coming off Marnie and aiming at me. "But Laurel could be wrong. She could be wrong about Halloween and pumpkins on the porch . . . things like that."

"Laurel is real smart," Marnie said. "You'd like her to be your girlfriend, wouldn't you?" Trust a kid to cut right to basics.

". . . I might," I said, "but she could be wrong."

"No. She's like Diana. She's real smart."

"Just because she's older doesn't mean she knows everything. I'm older, and I don't know everything."

"You're a boy," Marnie said. But she was easing around to the refrigerator. When she started rooting in it for the lettuce, I put my goggles on.

By the time Mom and Dad came in, I had the beanie-weenie in the microwave. They seemed to be relieved to see Marnie and me working. We're all pretty good at smoothing things over. For a minute I thought we might smooth this over too.

Still, Diana wasn't home. She keeps busy, but she's never this late. When we sat down to eat, nobody had any table talk. I was trying to think of a safe topic and couldn't. The fork in Marnie's hand looked huge. It was

skating around in her beanie-weenie, but she wasn't
eating anything. "I don't want any more," she said.
"My tummy aches."

"Honey, your tummy doesn't ache," Mom said.

Diana blew in then with this week's copy of *The
Suburbanite* sticking out of her book bag. She dropped
it and slid out of her coat. "Sorry I'm late," she said
all in a rush. "I'd have called, but I was down in the
village at *The Suburbanite* office. After the AIDS meeting I wrote a short article. Even if *The Warrior* ran it,
which I doubt, it wouldn't come out till practically
Thanksgiving. So I had another idea. I got up my
nerve and took it down to a real newspaper. They
read it and said they'd use it. They're gutsier than I
thought. It's going to run next week. They're completely computerized down there."

So Diana the reporter had jumped over the school
newspaper, and Garth, to take her story to the community at large. Her face was pink from the walk home,
and she was looking pretty pleased with herself.

Marnie slipped out of her chair. "Laurel isn't ever
coming back, is she?"

"No," Mom said. "Laurel isn't coming back."

Diana had been reaching for the salad. Her eyes
widened.

"You sent her away." Now Marnie was looking at
Mom, hard, pulling away when Mom reached out to
her. "I'm not going to school tomorrow. Miss Rosen is
like you. She doesn't know the truth either. Tomorrow
she's going to pull down the shades and read us ghost
stories. That's evil. That brings back the dead. The

books she reads to us have bad secrets in them. I don't trust Miss Rosen. I'm not going to school."

Marnie turned and walked out of the kitchen. Mom scraped her chair back to follow, but then she didn't move.

Diana was frozen in place. "What on earth has happened?"

Mom and I told her. Dad was as quiet as I'd ever seen him. Marnie was special to him. He didn't play favorites, but she was special.

"Laurel has poisoned Marnie's mind," Mom said, "and I don't know why, and I don't know what it's done to her. I'll have to talk this over with Laurel's mother."

"It wouldn't help, Mom." Diana reached down for the copy of *The Suburbanite*. It's our regional weekly. On an inside page a story by the editor was headlined:

BOOKS ON RIDPATH READING LIST
CHALLENGED BY PARENT GROUP

Dad took the paper and read it out loud.

Books assigned by Ridpath Junior High School teachers have been attacked by a group calling themselves "Children's Rights Forum." They demand removal of several books from classrooms and the school library.

"We are not book censors," the group maintains in a letter sent to all area newspapers. "But our children's moral values are being undermined by the obscene and the occult messages in books they are required to read."

The books in question include Robert Cormier's *The Chocolate War,* because it contains "offensive language, sexual content, and cigarette smoking," and Anne Frank's *The Diary of a Young Girl.*

When asked for comment Ridpath principal Dr. Martin Ericson said, "Parents have a right to decide what their children read. Any student can be assigned an alternative reading. But parents have no right to decide what other students will or will not read."

The group's letter states that "we are parents drawn together only to combat this conspiracy to mislead our children," though they all identify themselves as members of a prayer group meeting at Woodfield Community Church.

A parent asked for her comment, Mrs. Ben Kellerman of Highmeadow Drive, Walden Woods, said, "It is dangerous enough that children are brainwashed by the supernatural, witchcraft, devil worship, and heathen Halloween decorations throughout their gradeschool years. At Ridpath they're being assigned Anne Frank's diary that clearly asserts all religions are equally valid. These are not my values. These are not the values of my son."

A meeting of Ridpath faculty and the parent group is planned for eight o'clock Monday evening at the school.

We sat there. Diana was watching Mom. "So there's not much point in calling Mrs. Kellerman," she said. "It sounds like Laurel's talking in her mother's voice."

I couldn't believe it. Laurel's mother was a little birdlike woman with this quiet, kind of anxious voice. Now Laurel, this new Laurel, was whispering in my ear again, "Satan is everywhere, and his followers are here. . . . Are you that blind?"

And her brother, Billy, the one with the values, who hot-wires cars. He came to mind.

"These people," Mom said, "they can't mean this."

"Let's go up to Marnie, Mom," Diana said, pushing her plate back. "If we leave her alone, she's still with Laurel in a way."

Diana was mad. I know the signs. She was propping her hair behind her ears. Somebody had gotten to her little sister, and Diana was mad as the . . . devil.

You don't mess with her when she's like this. She blacked my eye once in fourth grade, I don't remember why, and was only sorry later. As she brushed past my chair, she said, "It looks like you got off easy, Todd. I wish Marnie had been that lucky. Maybe Laurel had us all fooled, but you really wanted to be fooled."

That got to me, though, I repeat, you don't mess with her in that mood. But Dad said, "Diana."

She turned back to him, and her eyes were crackling.

"What about me? Have you got some blame for me?"

"Dad, you hardly knew Laurel."

"But I should have. She was somebody coming into our house. I'm supposed to make this house safe for my family. But I took things for granted. I thought we lived in this civilized, safe place. I thought that's why we were here. Maybe I wasn't doing my job for all of us. I think we'd better stick together."

Tears welled up in Diana's eyes, and you don't see that every day either. "I'm mad at myself," she said in a low voice. "Laurel did a job on Marnie, and I probably helped. Marnie looks up to me and wants to be me, and I'm running around and don't give her enough time. She's a little kid, and she'd believe anything from somebody she looked up to. If *I* told Marnie her teacher was a witch, she'd believe it—just to please me.

"Sorry, Todd," she said, bumping my shoulder. Then she followed Mom out of the room.

It was still my meal. I thought about loading the dishwasher. Finally Dad said, "You liked Laurel."

"I guess I didn't know her. I guess I won't now. Mom's pretty upset about this. She wouldn't want me seeing Laurel even if—"

"When you're fifteen, why is everything always the parents' fault?" Dad said, smiling for the first time all evening.

I shrugged. "I don't know. I'm only fifteen."

"I was around that age when I read Anne Frank's diary." Dad held up the newspaper. "There was a movie too. I still remember the sound of the sirens when the Nazis were coming for the Frank family."

"According to the paper, Laurel's mother wants to ban that book," I said. "Parents again."

"I wouldn't want to see that book taken out of schools just because it wasn't about people who go to the same church I do. Would you?"

"No. Laurel's mother—"

"And Laurel too," Dad said. We sat there awhile longer, quiet.

Then he said, "Okay, here's the plan. We sell the house and move. The world's full of suburbs, and every one of them claims to have the best school system. You kids can start over and make all new friends. It'll be . . . cool."

The nightmare of starting in a new school with another bunch of strangers washed over me. Then I noticed Dad watching me out of the corner of his eye.

"Dad, this is no time for jokes. Make your point."

"My point is that we've already done that. We came here to get away from problems. We thought Walden Woods was as good as it looks. That was pretty naive. Places are like people; they're never quite what they seem to be."

"Like Laurel, I suppose. Does this mean we'd better not trust anybody?"

"It means we pull together as a family, no matter where we are. It means we find ways of reassuring Marnie without overreacting. She's wise. She'd see through that. It means life isn't as easy as we wanted it to be."

We got quiet again, and then Dad helped me load the dishwasher.

Later on I tried calling C.E. After six rings I got his voice recording. "This is C. E. Van Meter. I'm out right now, down at the barn slopping the hogs. If you'd care to leave your name and number and an easy-to-understand message, I'll get back to you."

I left no message.

Then in the night, toward morning, Marnie screamed again, that sound out of dead silence. I hit the floor. Mom and Dad were already in her room when I got there. Marnie was up on her knees on the bed, and her closet door was tight shut with a lot of toys stacked against it. All around the room the button eyes of animals winked in the light.

Marnie's arms were out, so Mom went into them and held her. I could remember that—how when I was little and fell off my tricycle or whatever, Mom was there. But Marnie was looking over her shoulder. "Where's Diana?" she said, wanting all of us.

Diana ran in, wearing the oversize sweatshirt she sleeps in. "We're here," Dad said, putting an arm around Diana's shoulder, an arm around mine. "We're all here."

Marnie sobbed one more time, and Mom put a hand on her forehead. But she wasn't sick.

"You don't believe," Marnie said to all of us, "so if you die, you're lost. And I won't be able to find you."

Chapter

Nine

Friday was Boo Day at school, when we make a joke out of Halloween. No grunt turned up in costume, because in tenth grade we really didn't want to be kids. But a few juniors and seniors tested the limits with some bizarre outfits.

Greg Wilcox, junior, was sent home for wearing full-body blue spray paint and not a lot else. Dwayne Reasoner, also a junior, turned up in a wig and blood-soaked shroud and fake facial wounds. Rumor was he was being the late Tara Lawrence, but nobody could pin it on him, and he stayed. Boomer Holmberg appeared as a two-hundred-and-forty-pound Madonna with what looked like two traffic cones on his chest, and also not a lot else. But nobody sent him home either. He's Conference All-Star material.

Most of the AIDS Awareness posters for yesterday's meeting were down, and the school halls were draped with toilet paper. The big moment of my morning was when cool Pace Cunningham stopped me between second and third period.

"Tad," she said.

"Todd."

"Todd, have you seen Diana?"

"I haven't, Pace." Pace Cunningham, junior star who probably doesn't even talk to junior guys, is talking to me, and I'm wondering how many people are picking up on this. I drag out my answer to give them time to notice. "I'm not fully briefed on her A.M. schedule, Pace, but she's definitely in school, because we arrived together. She was looking good when I saw her last."

Pace blinked. "Fine. Well, listen, if you see her, tell her she's in charge of picking up our Fortnightly Club Christmas dance posters from the printer. I want those posters up next week, as soon as this Boo Day madness is over."

"Be glad to, Pace," I said, but she was already moving out. "Say, Pace. What's the status on your Capri? Is it still in the shop, or do you have it back?"

"What?" She was looking past me. "Oh. No, they're still working on it, but I've got a rental."

"Good to see you, Pace," I said to her retreating back.

C.E. popped up just before lunch. Then inside the lunchroom so did Diana, who didn't have lunch this period. She was out of some class.

"Only gym," she said, reading my mind. "Where is she?"

"Pace?"

"Not Pace. Laurel."

"She's right over there," C.E. said.

Laurel was coming through the line, carrying her tray. This was the first day I hadn't been looking for her, and I didn't know what I'd say to her if I ran into her. She was lowering her tray onto a table when she looked up to see Diana.

"In case you care, Marnie's going to be fine, Laurel. She's still pretty upset, and we were up in the night with her again. Since you told her that the rest of us were going to hell because we don't believe in your weirdness, Marnie's scared that she'll lose us."

A vein was throbbing in Diana's temple, a well-known danger sign. And she was leaning over Laurel now, with the heel of her hand planted next to Laurel's tray. "You must feel pretty good about this, Laurel. Scaring the hell out of kids is probably a pretty important part of your religious life, right?"

Laurel wasn't looking up, wasn't moving. "I wasn't trying to scare Marnie," she said. "I just didn't want to watch a child falling into the devil's hands, doing the devil's work. Little kids don't know how danger's lurking everywhere."

"You're the danger," Diana said. "I call what you did child abuse."

"You probably would," Laurel said, sounding surer. "You're that blind. You're that lost. You think nothing could touch you. Nothing bad has ever happened to you in your perfect life. You're like these other people." She jerked her head around suddenly. "You're like the other girls around here. You have it all, and you know it all—you think."

After a long moment Diana said, "That's right, Laurel. Nothing bad has ever happened to me in my whole life. But it's pretty clear that something terrible has happened in yours. And it's not devils and witches and books on the shelf. You've got a problem, and it's all yours. You ought to go for help, and you ought to take your mother with you."

"We have help." Laurel almost met Diana's eye. "Our Christian beliefs. The church is the center of our lives. It's the last safe place there is. It's the only true church." She look around the cafeteria again. There was some food in the air. Boomer Holmberg as the giant Madonna strolled past with his people.

"God bless you," Laurel said to Diana, and looked away.

Diana turned, almost running down me and C.E. "She's totally programmed. This isn't worth cutting gym." I thought she was out of there then, but she whirled around toward Laurel again and planted her hand on the table.

"But hear this, Laurel," she said in almost a conversational voice. "I'm not Todd, and I'm not a teacher. I don't fight fair with people who fight dirty. If I ever see you near my sister again, it'll take more than religion to save you."

She slapped her hand on the table and was gone, elbowing C.E. and me out of the way.

I couldn't let things be like this. I had to do or say something. C.E.'s eyes were huge. "Go on through the line," I told him. "I'll catch up with you later." He left, but he was as curious as he gets.

I was standing over Laurel now, and I didn't know where to begin. "Listen, Laurel, for one thing, you shouldn't have said what you did to Diana. About how nothing bad ever happened to her, about how she's had a perfect life. You don't know her that well."

I wanted Laurel to look up. She didn't, but she was listening. She sat with her hands arranged in her lap, waiting for me to leave.

"Because Diana's life hasn't been all that perfect. Her parents, her real ones, died when she was small. That's something she's always had to deal with."

At least she was looking up at me. "So then she came to live with your family, and things were perfect for her." Laurel spoke in her usual voice, convincing and reasonable. "She shouldn't have said I'd abused Marnie. She doesn't have any right to use words like that. When I was little like Marnie, we went to a church like yours. I didn't want Marnie to be that help-less."

I knew I couldn't argue with Laurel or change her mind. But I couldn't give up either. "Look, a minute ago Diana lost it because she feels a little bit guilty about not showing Marnie enough attention. Then you come in and—"

No, that wasn't going to work either. My mind was gunning and going nowhere. But it didn't matter. Laurel reached for a napkin and unfolded it. She bowed her head, saying grace silently in this room of pounding sound. Then I went.

But I looked back. And she was sitting by herself, holding herself so carefully at a table full of strangers. She was perfect, and scary—what she'd done and the way she'd done it, so quick and quiet. It scared me, and I didn't like being scared, and I couldn't believe how wrong everything had gone.

After I got through the line, I found C.E. at a table at the far end of the room. "You want to put me in the picture about all this?" he said. "You want to fill me in?"

Telling him took the rest of lunch. Luckily, he didn't ask me how I felt about it all, because I didn't know. I never got around to asking him where he'd been last night when I called.

On Fridays we had English in the afternoon. We'd already wound up our discussions on *Fahrenheit 451*. I'd managed to get it read, and it had a pretty strong ending. The mind-control people have really taken over, and the people who still believe in books are fugitives. They're on the run, and in a way they've lost. But among them they've memorized the books. Their minds are the libraries nobody can burn.

Chance MacEnroe came in with the article on the Ridpath censorship case. Mrs. Lensky looked pleased and said, "Is there just one newspaper reader in this room?" I'd read it, but since none of the other guys said anything, I didn't. She read it aloud to us.

People reacted. Not a lot of book lovers in the class, but we all had a laugh about *The Chocolate War* containing "offensive language, sexual content, and cigarette smoking." Like you had to read a book to find out about these things.

Then when we heard the part about Laurel's mother condemning Anne Frank's diary because it "clearly asserts all religions are equally valid," everybody knew why Mrs. Lensky had brought up the book the other day.

"Wait a minute," Chance said. "This doesn't make any sense. The Frank family were being persecuted because they were Jews. The book didn't make any judgment calls about other religions. What's going on here?"

In the cafeteria Laurel had just said that her church was the only true church. Something must have shown in my face, because Mrs. Lensky was waiting for me to say something.

"Some people have strong religious beliefs," I said. "Maybe they don't want their kids—maybe anybody's kids—to know what other religions believe."

Chance MacEnroe turned on me like a Texas twister. "We're talking public schools here, Tobin! Public schools. Supported by everybody's taxes. Are we going to end up with public schools dictated by one church full of book-banners?"

Mrs. Lensky gave me time for an answer I didn't

have. Then she went on reading the article. When she'd finished, she looked up.

"Why do these people say they aren't book censors?" somebody asked.

"Book censors usually say that," Mrs. Lensky said.

We talked about *The Chocolate War,* and then we got into Anne Frank's diary. People remembered liking these books, even people who'd forgotten them till now.

"You can find something wrong with any book a teacher assigns, if you're looking," Neil Beaman said. "How come they picked these?"

"They take them from lists circulated by organizations," Mrs. Lensky said.

We had a pretty good discussion, for us, for a Friday afternoon. Toward the end of the period Brad Ellerby said, "Is that it? Is this our censorship project? I mean, Chance found the article, and we've talked it over. Is that it?"

"This is more than a discussion topic," Mrs. Lensky said. "This is about the community where you live. Some of you went to Ridpath. You read these books. Where do you stand, and what are you going to do about it?"

"We could go to that meeting on Monday at Ridpath," Chance said.

"Shut up, Chance," somebody said.

"Is it open to the public?" Cindy said. "Because it didn't exactly say that in the article."

"It didn't say it isn't," Mrs. Lensky said. "The Children's Rights Forum people will be there in force.

They're very well organized and led. They may count on being the only ones there."

Then somebody asked, "Are you going, Mrs. Lensky?"

"Turn up and find out," she said.

"Do we have to go?" said Nick Linstrom, who wouldn't be going anyway. "Is it required for this class?" And the bell rang.

After school I fell into my routine. The locker stop, and then my feet headed toward swim practice. After that I'd get home before Laurel left, and we'd—

But Laurel wouldn't be there. The afternoon vanished into a black hole. I tried thinking about girls in general, an old fantasy that had always worked, but didn't now. I wasted some time blaming Diana for attacking the girl I was probably in love with. And Marnie. Maybe we'd overreacted. Kids get scared by things, and kids bounce back. That didn't work any better than the fantasy thing. By then I was on a bench in the locker room.

But I retied my shoes and started for home. That may have been the day I quit swim team.

Mom had let Marnie stay home from school, because she wasn't ready to hear ghost stories and see Halloween costumes. At dinner Diana said, "I saw Laurel at school today."

Marnie looked up. "Did you say bad things to her?"

"I was pretty mad because she'd scared my sister, right?" Diana said. "I told her I wasn't going to hell just because she said so. I told her she needed help."

But Marnie wasn't sure about anything.

That was our night to watch *The Wizard of Oz*. We were all in the den with the popcorn, Marnie on Dad's lap. She was okay through the black-and-white Kansas part with Aunty Em and Dorothy in her regular shoes. But even before the tornado blows Dorothy away to the Yellow Brick Road, Margaret Hamilton shows up. She's not a witch yet, but she steals Toto the dog.

Marnie never had been too happy about that part anyway. She buried her face in Dad's chest. But he held her and recited the lines along with the characters, doing his best work as the Cowardly Lion. Marnie went sound asleep, and after the show Dad carried her up to bed. Halloween was the next day.

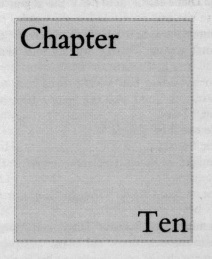

Chapter

Ten

Dad and I were up early to clear the leaves out of the gutters. He steadied the ladder and sent up advice. I like heights. As late as third grade I was going to be an astronaut. I scooped leaves down from the roof all morning, and Marnie raked below, working near us.

At dinner Dad said, "We're going to have trick-or-treaters tonight. There are going to be some ghosts and goblins around here wanting their popcorn balls."

"They shouldn't be out," Marnie murmured. "They better be careful."

"The little ones will be there with their parents," Dad said, but Marnie didn't like the sound of any of this.

"I think I'll wear a false face tonight," Diana said.

"Don't go out, Diana," Marnie said, shaking her head.

"I'm not going out. I want to be here to see the trick-or-treaters. Todd, you can wear a false face too."

"Not," I said.

"We could be clowns."

"Not," I said.

"I might work up a costume myself," Dad said, suddenly inspired.

"Not," Diana said. "Tonight you just be Dad, Dad."

The next thing I knew, Diana and Marnie and I were up in the bathroom, and Diana was painting red circles on my cheeks and stippling in big freckles. Diana made herself up, too, and she found a couple of red plastic noses from somewhere. We were only clowns from the neck up. Marnie sat on the edge of the bathtub, taking all this in. She was old enough to know we were doing this because of her, but when I got a big mouth on and grinned at her, she grinned back.

The popcorn balls were in a punch bowl, and Marnie sat a little way up the stairs. The first trick-or-treaters were little kids with their parents. Mom and Dad made a point of talking to the parents, and we overdid it in praising the costumes. Marnie's school friend, Gina, came as a ballerina, in leg warmers.

Later, some bigger kids in gross rubber heads

showed up without parents, but Marnie kept fairly cool. After the trick-or-treat rush hour we all went into the den to make a dent in the leftover popcorn balls. Diana and I plucked off our noses.

Popcorn reminded Dad of C.E. "Where is he? I can't remember a Halloween when C.E. wasn't here."

In the kitchen I punched up his number, but he hadn't activated his phone message, and nobody picked up. When he wasn't home, his mother usually answered, though she was blurry over the phone. She was a little blurry in real life. Suddenly I wanted to know where C.E. was.

"He's not out Halloweening by himself, is he?" Dad asked. C.E. was warped, but not that warped. Dad and I decided to drive over to his house.

There were a few pumpkin faces out on steps along Mill Lane to show the way, and the Van Meters' house was blazing with light as usual. C.E. himself was just coming across the yard toward the house as we pulled in the drive. He ambled over and leaned into the car. "You guys want to go for a hot dog and some Snapple?"

"Where you been, C.E.?" I said.

"Around."

"C.E., is your mother home?" Dad said.

"As a matter of fact, she isn't, Mr. Tobin." He started to reach out to shake Dad's hand, but didn't.

"Where is she?"

C.E.'s head dipped. All you could see was the point on the top of his sweatshirt hood against the glare of the lights from the house.

"She's in the hospital," he said. "I had to take her there the other night. You guys picked me up when I was walking home."

"But you didn't tell us that," Dad said.

"It's fine, Mr. Tobin. I could handle it."

Dad gave the steering wheel a bump with the heel of his hand. "C.E., you didn't have to handle it alone. You could have told us. What's the matter with your mother?"

I knew. I almost nudged Dad to keep him quiet.

"She's drying out," C.E. said in a kid's voice, not his own.

"Has she had to be in the hospital before?" Dad asked.

C.E. nodded. "I've had to take her a few times."

Now Dad had a question for me he didn't ask. Had I known this? I had and I hadn't. I knew Mrs. Van Meter drank a lot. I didn't know she'd had to go to the hospital, and C.E. had had to take charge of everything and then come home to this empty house. We're talking about my best friend here, but what did I really know about his life?

"So anyway . . ." C.E. said, his voice tapering off.

"Go in the house, C.E., pack some clothes, turn out all the lights, lock up, and bring the key," Dad said. "You're coming to stay with us."

C.E. wanted to. But he hesitated. "Mr. Tobin, I don't have too many clean clothes."

"We'll throw them in the washer."

C.E. turned back to the house, and I started to go with him to help him pack up, but Dad said, "No, stay here," in a voice a lot more serious than his usual. "Let him do it. He might not want you to see the shape the house is in."

"He keeps it in good shape," I said. "He vacuums."

"Downstairs," Dad said.

We sat there a minute. "How much of this did you know, Todd?"

"I didn't know C.E. was that much on his own."

"His dad?"

"He's never there. I've seen him maybe a couple of times in four years. They're not divorced or anything. Maybe they are. Maybe C.E. didn't tell me."

More time passed. The lights in the Van Meters' house began to go off.

"C.E.'s trying to be a grown man," Dad said, "because he's needed to be. But he's fifteen."

"I probably should have—"

"We all should have seen this. No kid's that cool. And he hangs around me because he doesn't have a father of his own. I should have seen that. I keep missing things about what's going on around here."

Dad's fist was bunched up, and he kept giving the steering wheel little punches. His wedding ring clicked.

"C.E.'s got a lot of pride," I said, realizing this.

"He needs more than that."

C.E. locked up the darkened house and came across the yard dragging a duffel bag and carrying a potted plant. It was an African violet or something. "This needs a lot of direct light," he said, climbing into the car.

When we came out of the dark into our kitchen,

C.E. got a good look at me and did a double take. My nose was off, but I was still a clown. Diana had washed her face, and she and Mom and Marnie were there, noticing C.E.'s duffel bag and watching him plant his potted violet on the windowsill.

Dad came in after us. "C.E.'s going to stay with us while his mother's in the hospital." Mom made a move toward C.E. when she heard that.

"We respect his privacy," Dad said. "But we want to help. His mother's being treated for alcoholism, and C.E.'s been coping with this for a long time. We didn't know. Now we do."

C.E. was looking smaller. He stroked his chin, gazed down, tried for his old-man image, and gave it up.

"C.E., how often have you had to take your mother to Lakeside?" Mom asked.

"A couple of times, Mrs. Tobin. I think the other night was the third time."

"Tell me about this."

"I usually take my mother in a cab. We go into Admissions, and they kind of know me by now. They call up her doctor. We usually have to wait a couple of hours till he comes around and gets her checked in. Sometimes she can sign the papers." C.E. shrugged. "Then I come home."

Mom thought about that. "The hospital people let you come home. They don't ask if anybody's at home for you. They don't ask you how you're getting home, even late at night. They just let you walk out."

C.E. nodded.

A look came over Mom's face. "I'm beginning to wonder about this wonderful, caring community we live in. With its car thieves and its hate groups and its superstitious book-banners and its full-service medical facility that will let somebody's son walk away without asking if he has anyplace to go. I'm beginning to wonder where we are and why we came here."

She turned to the rosters down the side of the refrigerator. "I'm not even so sure about these lists of ours. Maybe they mean we're not together enough."

Mom propped her hair behind her ears, that gesture Diana has borrowed. "I've never met your mother, C.E. I'm sorry about that. I should have."

"It's okay, Mrs. Tobin," C.E. said. "She doesn't see a lot of people. She doesn't go out much."

"I understand that," Mom said. "But I wish I'd known her all along. In a way we're neighbors. We live in this town. You and Todd are good friends."

"C.E. and I are good friends too," Diana said.

C.E. blinked. "Yo, C.E.," Marnie said in her version of teen-talk.

"What it is, Marnie?" he said.

"Stay till Christmas if you want to." She slipped a hand in his and got confidential. "Laurel scared me. Maybe you know."

"I heard something about it," C.E. said. "How you doing?"

"I'm hangin' in," Marnie said earnestly.

And now Mom looked like she was somewhere between laughter and tears.

C.E. settled in. He threw his laundry in with ours

and never missed a meal all weekend. He went into the other bed in my room, and sleeping in the same space took us back to Scout camp.

Sunday breakfast is Mom's job, with omelettes. C.E. noticed that Marnie liked watching him eat. She hadn't seen that much food vanish that fast, not even into me. As his fork took a plunge into the omelette, he muttered to her, "The last moments of Humpty Dumpty." Then he dug in.

He sat in church with us, filling out the pew. When he tried holding his hymnal upside down, Marnie helped with it. And when she waved at Diana up in the choir, so did C.E.

The three of us went off to school Monday. The censorship meeting at Ridpath was that night, and I decided to go. Maybe because we'd talked about it in Mrs. Lensky's class. Maybe because Laurel was still there in my mind, and I couldn't get her out, and didn't want her out.

Chapter

Eleven

C.E. decided to go to the censorship meeting with me. As we were leaving, Diana said, "I'll go too. Fortnightly meets tonight, but this is more important."

"Which reminds me," I said. "Pace Cunningham wanted you to pick up the Christmas Dance posters from the printer."

"She's already chewed me out about that," Diana said. "I may have more to do with my life than put up posters for Pace Cunningham." Snappy. Very snappy.

We'd just finished ninth grade at Ridpath last June.

Now it was like going back after years. The front doors
were open, but we didn't see people around. I thought
they'd hold the meeting in the auditorium with the
teachers up on the stage and the audience full of the
Children's Rights Forum, waving banners. I thought
they might even have to move it to the gym.

We wandered down an empty hall, smelling junior
high again. Mrs. Wilbraham came out of an office. We'd
all had her for eighth grade, and she was pretty much
everybody's favorite teacher. "It's great seeing you
three. If you've come for the meeting, it's in the library.
That seemed more fitting."

C.E. said, "We're on your side, Mrs. Wilbraham."

She smiled a little and said, "Isn't it too bad that
there have to be sides?"

There was no big crowd in the library. The principal, Dr. Ericson, sat at a table with Mrs. Tomlinson, the
librarian, and all the Language Arts and reading teachers. We'd had Mr. Horstman for seventh grade and
Mrs. Beal for ninth. Mrs. Wilbraham moved in with
them.

There were about ten other people in the room,
sitting grouped around a gray-haired man. They all
looked pretty average, and there weren't any banners.

"It looks like the PTA," Diana murmured.

Laurel's mother was there at the edge of her group
with a coat neatly folded over in her lap, the way she'd
been in the emergency room. She looked up and maybe
recognized me. Laurel wasn't with her.

Not too sure where we belonged, we perched on a
library table along one side. Chance MacEnroe and

three other girls from my English class came in and sat on the other side of C.E. Cindy Flagler hadn't made it.

Then Mrs. Dalbey came in, making one of her sudden appearances. The Children's Rights Forum people looked at her blankly. She hung there in the door.

Then from a chair at the back Mrs. Lensky stood up. "Mrs. Dalbey," she said in her classroom voice, "would you like to sit with me?"

But Mrs. Dalbey hesitated, giving the room one of her searchlight stares. Then she went around and sat next to Mrs. Lensky. It was pretty clear they weren't friends, but they were the only high-school teachers there. Then Mom and Dad came in, with Marnie.

"That was a last-minute decision," Diana said in my ear. A lot of Dad's outfits look like last-minute decisions, but Mom was just in jeans and a bulky sweater. She'd be pulled together better than this for the mall. They found chairs back behind Mrs. Dalbey and Mrs. Lensky. Marnie was checking out the scene with big eyes.

Dr. Ericson opened the meeting. In junior high I never gave the principal much thought unless I was being led into his office. He was tall enough to have played some basketball. Big hands. The way he talked, he might have had a minor in speech.

But before he could get going, a woman stood up from the Children's Rights group. She was quite a bit too old to have school-age kids. "Keep this in mind," she called out, holding up her Bible. "This is the only book we need in our schools. Keep this in your heart." She sat down, and even the Children's Rights people didn't look too comfortable with that. Still, they'd had the first word.

"We welcome the interest of parents," Dr. Ericson said. "We would welcome more parental support than we get. I regret that I haven't known more of you in this room tonight. I'm sorry our first meeting comes from your criticism, not your support. We have a big job to do with our students. They're at just the age when we've always lost most people to reading. And only readers have futures.

"We want them to read broadly and deeply. This school reflects the freedom of speech, thought, and inquiry guaranteed in the First Amendment of the United States Constitution."

But already another woman in the group was on her feet. "We aren't concerned with the First Amendment," she said. "We're concerned about our children."

"Do you think we aren't concerned about your children?" Dr. Ericson looked up over his glasses.

"I just don't know," she said. "If you taught the beautiful language of the classics instead of books that use filthy language to make our children hate their families and their country and their God, we'd support you. I've been in one of your classrooms. There are all kinds of books in shelves all over the walls. I thought I was in a bookstore, not a classroom."

She was looking at Mr. Horstman, who has the biggest classroom library at Ridpath. "We are only asking that you exercise some reasonable control over what our children read."

Mrs. Wilbraham spoke then. "Will you name a

book used in this school that you believe is danger-ous?"

The woman worked her mouth, then said in a lower voice, "Those books in our letter to the newspa-pers. That Anne Frank book. It's unchristian." She edged back on her seat.

Now Mrs. Dalbey stood up, tall in the room. "I'll tell you a dangerous book my ninth-grade son's class was forced to read." She ran a hand through her hair, and her voice rang out like it had that afternoon on Lombardy Lane.

"It was Paul Zindel's *The Pigman.* Some of these people here haven't even read the books they're ob-jecting to. But I read that book. It was full of disrespect for teachers and parents. The children in that book were out of control, and they suffered no conse-quences. It's a terrible book. I checked it out of the li-brary, and I'm not going to return it."

Her voice had climbed up and stopped. Mrs. Beal, next to the principal, said, "Are you Kevin Dalbey's mother?"

Mrs. Dalbey stiffened.

"I am Kevin's teacher," Mrs. Beal said. "Kevin didn't read that book."

Mrs. Dalbey looked like she wanted to sit down.

"And Kevin didn't ask me if he could read some-thing else instead," Mrs. Beal said. "I'd have recom-mended another book to him. He hasn't read anything in my class so far this semester. He hasn't handed in any written work. He's been absent as many days as he's been in class."

Mrs. Beal's hair was white. She may have been pretty close to retirement. And she had the room in the palm of her hand, whether they wanted to be or not.

"That isn't true," Mrs. Dalbey said.

"I keep accurate records," Mrs. Beal said. "I have to. You know that as a teacher yourself."

"Yes, I'm a teacher," Mrs. Dalbey said. "I wish everybody could see what goes on down at that high school. You ought to see those students riding roughshod over every rule of the school. Coming to class in nasty, obscene costumes and nearly naked. You ought to hear the language and the disrespect. They only come to that school to see their so-called friends. We're not teachers anymore. We're not allowed to be.

"A girl was killed this fall. Everybody read about it. A girl running around in the middle of a school night in a crowd of drunk kids, and she was killed. They ought to shut that school down. It's not doing anybody any good. I dread the day my boy has to go to that high school. I'm raising him on my own, and I'm doing the best I can. He doesn't need filthy books to undermine his moral code before he gets there."

Mrs. Dalbey's breath was coming hard. She looked at Mrs. Beal. "And what you said about my son. That isn't true. You are telling lies about my son." She sat down, and Mrs. Lensky beside her stood up.

"I'm a teacher at Walden Woods High School, too, one of Mrs. Dalbey's colleagues."

The Children's Rights Forum people stirred. The meeting seemed to be getting away from them.

"I teach English to tenth graders. We've just finished Ray Bradbury's *Fahrenheit 451,* a novel about the censorship of books and ideas. Later in the year I'll be assigning a story that involves suicide. It's about two sexually active teenagers whose parents disapprove. Some of the language is earthy. It's called *Romeo and Juliet.* A classic, I believe."

The Children's Rights Forum had heard about enough, but the teachers flanking Dr. Ericson were smiling. "In their junior year many of the students will be reading *Hamlet.* Those of you with superstitious beliefs must be reminded that the play begins with the ghost of Hamlet's father roaming the battlements of Elsinore Castle.

"We teach these great works because colleges expect students to be familiar with them. I mention that in case there are parents in this room who hope their children will be admitted to college."

Mrs. Lensky sat down. Chance MacEnroe leaned down our table. "Let's applaud," she said, and we did.

The gray-haired man at the center of the group stood up, and Dr. Ericson asked him to identify himself.

"I am Robert K. Enright," he said in a rolling voice that filled the room, "pastor of Woodfield Community Church. A number of these parents are members there, and I am with them merely as some small show of support.

"I only want to say how glad I am to be in this fine library." He made a sweeping gesture that took in the stacks of books around us. "After all, we are here to talk about books, and we've already drifted from the point. We are not here to discuss the curriculum and the conditions down at the high school."

He looked over at us sitting on the library table. Smiling warmly, he said, "And we certainly aren't here to listen to a group of enthusiastic teenagers trying to turn a serious meeting into a pep rally with their applause.

"And, Dr. Ericson, we don't question the goodwill of the Ridpath teachers. They deserve our prayers, and they are under influences beyond their control. They look as we do to their principal for moral leadership.

"We have no intention of allowing books in this school to destroy the innocence of children with their language and their unchristian messages. We hold Dr. Ericson responsible for upholding the standards we expect, in the clear understanding that his present contract as administrator here is up for renewal at the end of the year.

"This is a battle we will not lose, because right is on our side. God is on our side." Then he sat down.

Dr. Ericson was holding himself in now. "We have a procedure to be followed by any parent who questions a book." He held up a printed form. "You must identify yourselves and your affiliation with any group. You must complete this form indicating you've actually read the book you question, and you must describe your objections. Page by page. Line by line. Word by word.

"In a later faculty meeting we will evaluate these

forms. Our decision will be based on the merits of the book, not because of political pressure."

Beside me Diana said, "But none of this has to do with books, or Halloween. That's not what Laurel and her mother are about. That's not Mrs. Dalbey's problem either. It's not books that scare them."

"Then what?" I said.

But Chance was leaning past C.E. to say, "There's something really desperate about these people. They're huddling, and it's like they're just hanging on. They want control—bad."

Then she put up her hand, a classroom reflex. But nobody called on her, so she stood up. "As an enthusiastic teenager," she said with a slight drawl, "I'd just like to say how much I appreciated reading the books these people want censored. All of us were in ninth grade last year." She jerked a thumb back at us. "We had all kinds of problems in junior high, but none of them were about books. And if anybody had told us not to read a book, that's the first one we'd have read."

She settled back on the table, and the first lady who'd spoken looked over at us from the center of the group. "You young people ought to be at home this minute, with your families and your Bibles."

This brought Dad suddenly to his feet, popping up at the back of the room so fast that Marnie was still hooked around his neck. "Two of those young people are my children," he said, "and the others are their friends." He looked down at the Children's Rights people. "I know where my children are this evening. Do you?"

Dad seemed to provide the climax for the meeting. It began to wind down. Mrs. Tomlinson brought out the pile of forms. The Children's Rights Forum were standing now, turned in to each other. They were bowing their heads in silent prayer.

Then when they started to go, they left the forms on their chairs. Mrs. Dalbey crossed in front of us, heading for the door with her long stride.

From the teachers' table Mrs. Beal called out, "Mrs. Dalbey? I'll be glad to talk further to you about your son. I'd appreciate a parent conference." But Mrs. Dalbey was gone by then.

I was dazed by the whole thing. Nobody had really heard anybody else. You kind of hoped grown people would act better than this.

Mrs. Kellerman had stood with her eyes closed a little longer than the others. She didn't seem to relate that well to her own people. Now she was unfolding her coat with all those gestures Laurel had inherited.

Dad and Mom and Marnie came up from the back of the room, talking with Mrs. Lensky. You could hear Dad from here. "I can't believe I heard a minister of a church threatening a school principal for doing his job. I can't believe I heard that."

Mrs. Kellerman was still there, and some circuit went haywire in my brain. I slipped down off the table and went over to her. She was almost within reach.

"I'm Todd Tobin," I said. This was the kind of thing Diana would do, not me. I sensed her behind me, still on the table.

"Yes, of course I know you, Todd." The ghost of a smile crossed Mrs. Kellerman's face.

"I'd like you to meet my parents." They were right there behind me. And maybe I thought I could solve this whole business right here. "This is Laurel's mother," I said, and she was smiling, at Mom and Dad.

Mom didn't put out her hand to Mrs. Kellerman. She reached down and touched Marnie's shoulder.

"This is Marnie," Mom said. "I'd hoped your daughter would be a good companion for her. She wasn't."

The bottom went out of my world when I heard that. But Marnie was there, so Mom couldn't let this escalate into a major scene. Mrs. Kellerman looked suddenly aside, but Reverend Enright was gone. "I'm sorry you think that," she said. "My daughter means everything to me. Everything. She's a lovely, God-fearing girl. The baby-sitting money was important to her. My husband is out of work. He lost his job soon after we came here, and so things are hard for us. He wouldn't like me telling our private business, but I'm telling you, though I'm sure you couldn't understand."

Diana was still behind me, and I couldn't hear her breathing.

"Your daughter came into my house and terrorized my child. Now I'm to pity her because your husband is out of work?" Mom said. "No, I can't understand that."

Mrs. Kellerman looked down and then up again and said, " 'The God of this world hath blinded the minds of them which believe not.' "

Then she walked away.

Marnie had hold of Mom's hand and Dad's. "I miss her, though," she said. "I miss Laurel."

Mom and Dad took her home in the car, but Diana and C.E. and I wanted to walk. I for one needed some fresh air bad. So it was the three of us going along through the nippy November night, skirting Founders Park. This must have been the first time in history C.E. didn't suggest going for a pizza or a taco or something. Maybe because he was eating regular meals now.

"The trouble is," I said, "there's no give in anybody's position. Nobody gives an inch because they're all so sure they're right. Even Mom."

"Don't start on Mom," Diana said.

"I'm not. I just didn't know she could be that . . . fierce."

"I'll be that fierce," Diana said, looking far ahead into some future. "Believe it. And don't mope."

"Me? Who's moping? Am I moping, C.E.?"

"I can't tell. It's dark out here," said C.E., who may be turning into a diplomat.

"There are worse things around here than not finding a girl. Lots worse things. Besides, you'll find one," Diana said. "Sooner or later."

The spot in my mind where Laurel had been was beginning to shrink, a little, but it was still tender to the touch. And now the moon came out, which didn't help. But I was scuffing along through the leaves on a crispy night with C.E. and Diana. Which was okay too.

It was good, just not quite how I'd pictured high school.

Chapter

Twelve

We were on our countdown to Homecoming that week. The Halloween toilet paper was gone, and the school halls were hanging in yellow and green crepe paper, Warrior colors.

On Wednesday Diana and Garth Lashbrook got into a major dustup in the main hall of school. Garth's in his usual steel-rimmed glasses and broadcloth shirt. He's carrying an attaché case that no doubt holds his cellular phone. The guy is about a hair from being a dork, if you ask me. But he's got some kind of preppie glamor for girls.

Now here he is at the main intersection of school up in Diana's face with a copy of that day's *Suburbanite,* the issue with her AIDS Awareness article in it. I came on this scene purely by accident.

"Look, Diana," he was saying, "can we talk over this piece you wrote?" Garth was heating up under his button-down collar. His Adam's apple was doing a little dance.

"I think it speaks for itself." Even from here you could see there were two Dianas in this proceeding. One was the Diana who had a semisecret yearning for Garth. The other Diana takes nothing from anybody, let alone about something she's written. I personally thought Garth ought to exercise some caution here.

"Diana, listen," he said. "*Warrior* staff members write for *The Warrior.* Right? And another thing, which I'm telling you for your own good. The piece you did could use some editing. Frankly, it didn't make this school look particularly good."

"You don't mean editing," Diana said, strangely calm. "You mean censoring."

"I don't mean censoring. I mean you write for us, not *The Suburbanite.* And until you've got some experience under your belt, you wait for an assignment. Diana, we're not a bunch of free-lancers running . . . amok."

"But you didn't assign anybody to cover the AIDS Awareness meeting," Diana said. "Did you, Garth?"

Walk away, Garth, I thought.

"You want to tell me why you didn't assign anybody to cover that meeting?" she said.

"Priorities," he said after a second. "We only come out every two weeks, and we can't cover everything. You know this isn't completely my decision, Diana. You know we have staff meetings."

"I wish you hadn't brought up those staff meetings. I was trying to forget. I found out what the priorities were at the first staff meeting. Half *The Warrior*'s given to covering football season, because you're afraid not to. You don't want the coaches on your tail."

That was a bit below the belt, though true.

"Garth, tell me something that happens around this school more important than a meeting about AIDS. You've already slotted a personality profile on Boomer Holmberg that never quite mentions he was breaking training by being out in that van Tara Lawrence was killed in.

"I'm sure everybody in school is immune to AIDS, or they think they are," Diana said. "So if it's not happening to us, it's not happening. Right? Garth, I wanted the newspaper to be better than that."

His hand slipped under her elbow. "Diana, you're an idealist. And that's good. That's important. When I was your age, starting out on the paper—"

She jerked away from him. "Give me a break, Garth! You're only about twenty-four months older than I am. We're both just a couple of high-school kids. You don't even need to go to Harvard. You're already pompous enough."

Ouch, I thought. But Garth hung in there, and I

gave him credit for that. His hand was reaching around for her elbow again. "Okay," he said. "I know I can be a little . . ."

"Pompous."

"Pompous. Let's just put this on hold till after school. Then we can talk it over, just the two of us, no staff meeting. We'll go out for coffee somewhere."

This was almost asking for a date. But Diana said, "I think we're all talked out."

She turned away, and she'd let him off easy. One thing that seemed to steam Garth was that tenth-grade Diana had gotten an article in a real newspaper, and he never had. But she let that go. I thought she was going to walk away. Maybe it was easier for her to walk away from people and situations than it was for me. But she looked back once before the crowd swallowed her up.

In English Mrs. Lensky had a copy of *The Suburbanite*. We'd been wondering what we were going to do now that we'd finished up *Fahrenheit 451*—whether or not we'd be going right into *Romeo and Juliet*. She started by reading Diana's article aloud.

AWARENESS OR APATHY?
AIDS MEETING
HELD AT WALDEN WOODS HIGH SCHOOL
by Diana Tobin

An AIDS Awareness meeting was held at the high-school library last Thursday, sponsored by librarian Mrs. Lillian Noyes.

Speakers included a research physician, two members of a support group providing meals to homebound AIDS sufferers in urban neighborhoods, and a reporter for a national news magazine who is herself HIV positive.

The speakers dispelled many myths about AIDS and described the testing, services, and counseling for patients and the HIV positive, urging compassion for people living with the illness and for their families.

A publicity campaign for the meeting had filled the halls of WWHS with posters. Except for six teachers and Mrs. Noyes, no student attended apart from this reporter. The only other students in evidence were in the hall outside, one of them a senior who made a homophobic remark.

"The administration agreed to this meeting only if we held it after school and made attendance voluntary," Mrs. Noyes explained. She apologized to the speakers for the size of the audience. "We make even the issue of AIDS optional for our young people, and in the long run that could cost many of them their lives."

Mrs. Lensky finished reading and looked at us over the paper. The word *homophobic* had gotten a small rise out of Brad Ellerby, though he'd only picked up on the first two syllables. Now people in the class seemed to be doing various things. Cindy had been rummaging around in her purse and was retrieving her lip gloss from the floor. For the first time this year Nick Linstrom kicked off the discussion.

"There was a guy with AIDS in this school?" I hadn't seen him this alert before.

Mrs. Lensky looked puzzled, but Chance got it.

"The reporter," she said, smiling at Mrs. Lensky, who rolled her eyes.

She read that part again, about "a reporter for a national news magazine who is herself HIV positive."

"A woman?" Nick looked around like none of this made sense.

"And HIV positive," Chance said.

"What's the difference between that and AIDS?" Nick said.

"If you'd been at the meeting, Nick, you'd know," somebody muttered—somebody who hadn't been at the meeting either. He gave his little sneer and kicked back in the seat.

"They shouldn't make meetings like that voluntary if we need to know this stuff," Cindy said, and a few people agreed.

"It would have been a better article if it had repeated all the information they gave at that meeting," Neil Beaman said, casting me a glance because my sister wrote it. "Then we'd know without having to go."

Mrs. Lensky glanced at me too. "I don't think that's the point of this article. Do you, Todd?"

I might have known I was going to get pulled into this. "No. Knowing Diana. The news in this article is that they gave a meeting about AIDS, and none of us went."

A little more silence, and then somebody said, "You went to the meeting, didn't you, Mrs. Lensky?"

"Of course."

"Then you can tell us about it."

"I don't think I can," she said. "A woman was there, my age, counting every moment of her life because she's HIV positive. I can't describe it. You had to be there."

The clock jumped another minute, and Brad Ellerby said, "Is that it? Are we going to be doing an AIDS unit? Is that what we're building up to here?"

"No, we're still on the censorship topic," Mrs. Lensky said. "It takes a lot of forms."

The clock jumped again, and Chance said, "I think I see the censorship angle here. The administration wouldn't let the meeting be on school time, and it had to be optional. They were afraid parents or some group would come down on them if they made learning about AIDS a required event. This time the administrators were the censors."

It was a thought. But Mrs. Lensky said, "Still, the school did approve it as an after-school event. But it was for you, and you turned away. You don't like it when other people try to keep you from ideas. But you did it to yourselves. This time you people are the censors."

"Whoa," somebody said, and the bell rang.

C.E. and I walked home that afternoon, our new routine. Mom was hanging around in the kitchen, waiting for us. As C.E. eased nearer the refrigerator, she reached out and put an arm around his shoulder. Then she told him the hospital had called, and they were letting his mother come home. He looked anxious, but ready.

"How do you want to do this?" Mom asked him.
"We'd like to take you and your mother home." C.E.
agreed. He packed up his duffel bag and collected the
African violet off the windowsill. Diana wasn't home
yet, so Marnie went with us.

C.E.'s mother was in the waiting room at Lakeside
with her stuff in a Nordstrom's shopping bag at her
feet. "Chucky?" she said, like she wasn't sure. Mom
had talked him out of his hooded-sweatshirt look, at
least for now. He was looking good in a Windbreaker
and a haircut. Not thinner, but a touch more mature.

His mom still had on that plastic ID bracelet they
make you wear in hospitals. Her hands were clasped in
her lap, and the wedding ring looked loose on her finger. She had a raincoat on, gaping open, and something
like a short nightgown on underneath. She seemed to
be pretty tired.

C.E. looked at her, stroking his chin. He hadn't
even been able to talk to her on the phone. They didn't
allow that while she was having her treatment. Then
he bent down to her and said, "Mother, I've been staying with the Tobins."

Her hand, like a little claw, came out and clutched
his. "Oh, I was worried about how you were getting
along. I worry." She looked up at Mom. "That was nice
of you. That was kind."

"We like having him," Mom said. "He's Marnie's
special favorite." She urged Marnie forward, and Mrs.
Van Meter smiled at her, though she wasn't really fo-
cusing. But Marnie didn't pull back. She understood
about C.E.'s mom.

Mrs. Van Meter wore flimsy slippers, and she shuffled when she walked. At the hospital door she looked back once. Then she and C.E. sat in the backseat on the way home. Before we were out of Hospital Drive, she thought she ought to make some conversation.

"I appreciate the ride. I don't drive myself anymore. I've only had three tickets, but after four they pull your license. They run you right off the road and tear it up in front of you. I had a friend that happened to, so I don't drive now."

When we swung into Mill Lane, Mrs. Van Meter said to C.E., quieter now, "I counted the minutes till I could come home. Now I'm scared." Then in a stronger voice, "I can't promise this will be the last time. I want to real bad, but I can't."

And I didn't hear anything from C.E., though I think he was holding her hand. It occurred to me that I was going to miss having him around the house. He was a brother of mine.

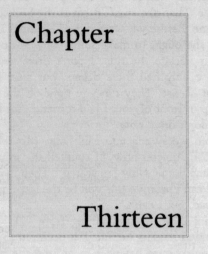

Chapter

Thirteen

We like a Homecoming game we can win, so this year
we took on the Diamond Lake Raiders, the smallest
school in the conference. We flattened them on a yel-
low-and-green football afternoon under a blue sky.
Boomer Holmberg covered his two-hundred-and-forty-
pound self with gridiron glory.

It was a great bonfire evening too. Shore Tent &
Awning had set up the hospitality tent between the
bonfire and the gym where the dance would be. To

honor the alums we served Coke in the classic green
bottles with the old-time crinkly lids that have to be
pried off. My job was to fish them out of the ice chests
and get the lids off with freezing fingers and hand them
over.

Misty, the other sophomore committee rep, didn't
show. But I'd foreseen that and deputized C.E. to help
me. The Cokes were free, so we kept busy all evening
and were rushed off our feet in the hour running up to
the bonfire. Once, Mrs. Dalbey, faculty advisor, drifted
by with her clipboard, but she could see we were tend-
ing to business and didn't say anything.

C.E. got into it. We wore the big plastic aprons
provided by Dominick Distributors, who'd donated the
Cokes. I wore my green-and-yellow WWHS ballcap,
backward. And I happened to notice C.E. was wearing
a new top-of-the-line work shirt I hadn't seen before.
He'd also rubbed some kind of semislick substance into
his scalp to fit his hair smoother to his head.

Finally the crowds were forming around the bonfire, this cone-shaped pile of kindling the size of a small
barn. The Walden Woods fire department stood by.
C.E. scooped the last Cokes out of the water and pulled
their lids.

At that moment Chance MacEnroe appeared out of
the crowd. "Chance . . . of . . . a . . . lifetime!"
C.E. said, and flourished a Coke across the counter to
her. "Looking good."

Until then I hadn't appreciated what a truly good
looking girl Chance MacEnroe was. Being Texan, she

was playing the role that night. Western-cut buckskin jacket with fringe and a big-brimmed cowboy hat with a pheasant-feather band.

She and C.E. swapped what sounded like a few pleasant insults, but I was hunkered down, draining the ice chests. I was also wondering how I could work my way into this conversation. But when I got my chests drained, C.E. already had his apron off. Then to my wondering eyes he planted a hand on the counter and sprang over it, landing next to Chance. I'd never seen C.E. leap a counter in a single bound, and I still couldn't believe it. It was weirdly like watching somebody jump higher than his own head. Now C.E.'s arm was draped around Chance's buckskin shoulder.

"Catch you after the bonfire and dance, maybe," he said to me, an octave below his usual range. I stood there amazed in my backward ball cap and my apron, working my frostbitten hands. They started to walk away.

"C.E.," I said, "a moment of your time, if you don't mind."

Chance waited, and he strolled back, propping an elbow on the counter.

"What it is, I mean, what is it, C.E.? What's happening? You. Chance. Talk to me."

He blinked. "We're going to the bonfire. We're going to the dance."

"Ah. C.E., we don't date around here. We're too cool."

"It's not a date," C.E. said. "I said to Chance, 'You

want to go to the bonfire with me? You want to go to the dance? It wouldn't be a date.' "

"And what did she say?"

"She said, 'Whatever.' "

"But you don't know how to dance."

"How do I know till I've tried?"

"C.E., you don't even know Chance. How do you know Chance?"

He blinked again. "I met her at that Ridpath censorship meeting. You were there. She sat on the table right next to me."

I stared back at him. "You work fast, C.E."

His innocent eyes returned my gaze. "I use the time."

They strolled away together. She was in cowboy boots. He was doing his duck walk. And the bonfire burst into flame. It was seeded with something that turned the flames purple and green and every color. The crowd made that low sound that comes out of people for bonfires and fireworks. The flames spiraled up, and you could feel a halo of warmth in the cold night air. Some of the alums began to sing the school song. We don't know the words anymore, but they remember them.

> Walden Woods school days,
> Too suddenly past,
> Walden Woods memories,
> Always to last,
> Walden Woods friendships
> To strengthen and grow,

Wherever life leads us,
Wherever we go . . .

The bonfire settled into a gigantic ember with a
heart of fire, glowing bright on the faces. I was out of
my apron, moving through the crowds to get up closer.
Then I spotted Diana and Mom and Dad. Marnie was
up on Dad's shoulders. We watched the bonfire burn
down together, the timbers glowing, then breaking up
and throwing sparks. By then the band was starting up.

Music coming out of a gym on a woodsmoky
night made Dad even more mellow than usual. Suddenly inspired, I said, "Let's go over and check out the
dance. We can sit up in the bleachers. It could be inter-
esting." I had C.E. and Chance in mind, of course.

We strolled across the campus, and the people
around us were of all ages, like you never see them in
Walden Woods. The gym glowed in front of us, and
Mom said, "This reminds me of my junior-senior prom
night."

"Who did you go with?" Diana said.

"Junior Steadman," Mom said. "He had an interna-
tionally recognized collection of Alice Cooper records."
Dad sighed. And Diana and I made a silent pact not to
ask who Alice Cooper was.

"Mother and Daddy came to sit up in the bleachers
and watch."

"Grandma and Grandpa Highsmith came to your
prom?" Diana stared. "They watched?"

We don't hold proms in the gym anymore. We
hold them in big downtown hotels. But tonight was

Nostalgia Night, and the gym girders were wrapped in school colors. We watched from the second tier as couples came out on the floor. The band alternated new music with old, making a long jump from Arrested Development to doo-wop. When they got back to prehistory, the gym floor filled up with jitterbuggers.

Mom leaned forward, elbows on knees, chin in hands, peering intently. "Do you see that girl down there in the cowboy hat? Who is that with her?"

Before our very eyes C.E. was learning to dance. He was on all sides of Chance, twirling her, twirling himself, flailing his arms around—developing a style. His feet were a blur, and the other dancers were giving them space. A circle of empty floor followed wherever they went.

And Marnie was up on the bleacher, yelling down at the top of her lungs, "Yo! C.E.!"

But I had to get back to the tent to crate up the empties so Dominick Distributors could pick them up.

"I'll give you a hand," Diana said, getting up and dusting herself off.

"Don't stay out too late," Mom said. Marnie was beginning to fade. Diana and I took giant steps down the bleachers and back outdoors, heading toward the silhouette of the tent against the glowing remains of the bonfire. It was still sending up sparks.

Diana stuck the bottles in the crates, and I stacked. "So it's just you and me, kid," she said. "Old C.E. has moved on and left us eating his dust. Who knew he'd be the first?"

"Might have known. He's sneaky. And Chance is a

fox." It didn't take us long to get our work done. Now
the fire department was hosing down the bonfire and
digging up the coals.

"You work steadier than C.E."

"But, boy, can he dance," Diana said.

We walked home on the usual route, skirting
Founders Park, because that's where the drug deals go
down. As she said, it was just Diana and me now,
hanging in there together. I'd thought that in high
school we'd really be going in different directions,
climbing separate trees. But things aren't the same
when you get there. It was like Diana and I were closer
than we'd ever been.

When we turned into the drive at home, the house
was lit up. Something was going on in the living room.

"They're at it again," Diana said. We crept closer
till we were practically in the shrubbery, where we
could see in the living-room window. Mom and Dad
were in there, dancing. The Homecoming dance must
have inspired Dad. The two of them were slow-danc-
ing around the living room. Mom's head rested on
Dad's shoulder, and he was making smooth moves
around the furniture. You couldn't see their feet, and so
they were floating. Mom was a little shorter than usual,
so she may have taken her shoes off. You couldn't hear
the music. I had an awful feeling it might be Harry
Connick, Jr. They do that sometimes. They go into the
living room, pop in a CD, and start swooping around.
The Fred and Ginger of Tranquillity Lane.

"I love that," Diana said. "I hope I do that."

We stood there watching for a while. Then, when we turned around, somebody was standing at the dark edge of the lawn. Diana reached for my arm. But it was okay. It was Laurel. Who else could stand there that quiet, that pulled in on herself?

Chapter

Fourteen

"I'm not supposed to be driving, but I know how." She nodded back at the shadowed drive, and that's when I saw the rear bumper of a car. "I had to take my mother to the hospital."

I couldn't find my voice, but I went over to her. Diana stayed where she was. And I think Laurel was watching her, keeping her distance too. I didn't want them to get into it again. I just wanted—

"I sat out in the car for a while," Laurel said in her

low voice. "I wanted to come up and ring the bell, but then I knew that wasn't a good idea. I was about to leave when I saw you come home."

"What happened to your mom?" I said, and Diana was closer behind me now.

"She's had some . . . injuries. To her face, her eye. Head injuries."

"You better come in the house," I said. "It's okay."

She shook her head, and she was looking past me at Diana. "No, I wasn't thinking straight when I came here. I'd just left the hospital, and I was afraid. . . . I didn't know where to go."

"Why not home?" Diana said.

"Diana, don't," I said. A wind came up, scraping the leaves in the gutters along the curb. "At least let's get in the car."

Laurel went into the driver's seat, and I thought she might just start up and reverse out of the drive before I could get around to the passenger's side. I slipped into the backseat, and Diana followed me in.

"Are they taking care of your mom at the hospital?" I said, to keep Laurel talking.

She nodded. I could barely see her in the dark. "I had her insurance card. I got her purse when we left home. She'll be all right. It's probably not as bad as it looks."

She dipped her chin down the way she does. Her hair was tangled like it never is. "Just tell us about it," I said, "like it happened."

After a moment she said, "It was Billy." She ran a

hand over the curve of the steering wheel. "You both know Pace Cunningham. Billy stole her car and wrecked it."

Her voice sounded worn out. "But tonight they got caught. The police picked them up trying to run away from a truck they'd piled up in a ditch somewhere. They brought Billy home, maybe because he said he was twelve. He's thirteen."

I could picture the cops bringing Billy home and Mr. Kellerman opening the door, filling it up, and seeing his kid caught.

"What did your dad have to say about that?"

"He wasn't home," she said. "He's . . . out of town."

"Looking for a job?" I said.

She made a quick turn back to me. "How do you know that?"

"Your mom told us he was out of work. At that censorship meeting at Ridpath."

Laurel sighed. "That's almost funny. Mother's so anxious that nobody should know anything about us, or our private family business. Then she tells it herself. My dad's desperate for a job, and that makes everything worse."

I felt her slipping away from us. "Go on," I said.

"The police brought Billy home. Two of them brought him up to the door. They had him by the arm, and he didn't like that. They told Mother they were releasing him in her custody and that he'd have a court date. All she wanted was for them to leave before the neighbors saw the squad car out front." Her voice wavered. "I wish they hadn't gone.

"Billy wasn't too concerned. Once the police let go of him, he was fine. He probably thought that since they'd brought him home, he'd won.

"He just headed off to his room. But Mother said something that . . . made him mad. I guess in a way she brought it on herself, because she knew she shouldn't say anything. She told Billy he was doing the devil's work, but it wasn't his fault. It was because of all those books they have to read for school. She said he was a good, God-fearing boy in his heart, if he'd only come to church with us.

"She didn't yell at him or anything. She never yells. If my dad had been there, she wouldn't have said anything at all.

"I thought Billy was just going to sneer at her the way he does when Dad's there. We were all still in the living room, and the Bible—our family Bible that belonged to my grandparents—it was lying there on the table. Billy grabbed it up and told Mother he'd show her what our church meant to him.

"He was going to tear up the Bible—rip it apart. Mother rushed at him to get the Bible back. That's all she meant. And he hit her."

Laurel's hand was over her mouth. She wasn't looking back at us, and her words were muffled, but we heard. "He just hit her and hit her. I tried to stop him, but he was crazy. And he's really strong. He kicked her once even, after she fell."

And now in the dark backseat Diana's hand was closed over mine, tight.

"He threw the Bible on the floor and went off to his room and banged the door. Mother was just lying there, sobbing and in awful pain but afraid to scream in case the neighbors heard. I had to get her to the hospital. Of course she didn't want to go, but she couldn't even speak. She just shook her head back and forth, and there was . . . a lot of blood. . . ." Laurel's voice trailed away.

"You wouldn't understand, but it's ironic in a way. We started going to this new church, Reverend Enright's, because of Billy. I see that now. Dad wouldn't do anything about him, and Mother couldn't. And so she wanted something strong to hang on to, something stronger than we are."

"But you came to us," Diana said.

"You were the only people I know. We haven't lived here very long."

But that didn't make sense.

"You and your mother go to a church," Diana said. "Your mother belongs to a prayer group and to that Children's Rights Forum bunch. And we're the only people you know?"

Laurel looked up. "But we couldn't go to them. What would they think? They're believing Christian people. They've been saved. What would people at church do if they knew that Billy's a . . . criminal? It would make us criminals, too, in their eyes. We'd be shamed. Don't you see that?"

"Maybe they wouldn't have tried to help you," Diana said. "Maybe they're all too busy trying to burn books and take over the schools. But there must be some members of your church who care. . . . They didn't all join that church because they've got troubles at home they're trying to hide. You didn't even give them a chance."

"I knew you wouldn't understand," Laurel said quietly. She sat up straighter and just touched her hair. She was about to start the car. "It's going to be all right," she said, mostly to herself. "I told the emergency-room people that Mother had fallen down the basement stairs."

"Laurel, they're not going to believe that," I said.

"And, really, I ought to be getting home. It's late."

"Laurel, you can't go home to Billy."

"It doesn't matter. He's probably not even home. He usually isn't."

"But he'll come back," I said, "and will your dad be home by then?"

"Is your dad ever coming back?" Diana said.

That tore it right there. I hadn't even thought about that.

Laurel put her face in her hands, and I reached past her to take the keys out of the ignition. She made no move.

"Now what?" Diana said, the edge still on her voice.

"She can't go home. You know that, Diana. Let's go in the house. Dad and Mom—"

"Your mother doesn't want me in her house," Laurel said, "any more than Diana does."

"No," Diana said. "I don't."

"Diana, forget about everything else. You know Laurel can't go home with Billy running around loose. We can't let her."

I didn't even know how to say it. Wasn't this our chance to prove to Laurel that we weren't . . . heathens? She didn't even think we were believing Christians. She'd just gotten that idea across. Maybe Diana was about to say that we didn't have to prove anything about ourselves to Laurel. "Diana—"

But she just said, "All right, let's go in the house and get this worked out." I wasn't too sure about what was going on in her mind. Still, this looked like a step in the right direction.

"We don't have to," Laurel said. "None of this is your problem. Todd, just give me the keys and I'll go."

But I wouldn't, and she didn't even reach back for them. We all climbed out of the car. The living-room windows were still lit up. Mom and Dad were still dancing, and I thought this was incredible. I thought we'd sat out in that car for hours. Years.

But there was something else I wanted to know. Laurel was standing by the car now—locking the door. "Who was the other kid?" I asked her. "The one Billy wrecks cars with?"

"Kevin Dalbey," she said.

And I suppose it made sense. I caught a couple glimpses of Mrs. Dalbey: that afternoon on Lombardy Lane, that night at the censorship meeting. She'd had trouble at home, too, and not even a group to hang on to.

I watched Mom through the window in the kitchen door. She was coming to unlock it, in her stocking feet, a little breathless from the dancing. She scooped a strand of hair off her forehead and checked her watch.

Then when she opened the door, she saw Laurel there with us. Laurel said, "You probably don't—"

"No. It's all right," Mom said. "Come in, Laurel. I always thought something would bring you back."

Dad came into the kitchen. Diana walked past him and out of the room. So it was only the three of us, and Laurel. We sat around the table in that pool of light. I got her to tell her story again. When she told what Billy had done to her mother, Dad looked down. But Mom's eyes never left Laurel's. She was trying to see beyond the words, the way you have to do with Laurel.

When she came to the end, we sat there, and I was still looking around for something that would make this right.

"I'm sorry about what you've had to live with," Mom told her. "You remind me of C.E."

I hadn't thought about that—how hard Laurel and C.E. both worked on their images so you couldn't see the problems underneath.

I didn't see why Laurel shouldn't stay with us for a while, until they let her mom come home from the hospital, or until her dad came home, if he was coming home.

"I'm going to bring Marnie down," Mom said, getting up. "She's only playing possum. She reads under the covers."

She came back, carrying Marnie. It was funny in a way, with Marnie's bare legs hanging way down. Mom had told her Laurel was here, because Marnie looked eager and curious. She hadn't been asleep.

"Hello, Marnie," Laurel said, and Marnie would have gone over to her, except she was in Mom's arms.

"I thought Laurel wasn't allowed to come back."

"I'm glad she has," Mom said. "I know you missed her. Laurel's family is having some bad troubles. We're sorry about that."

Marnie nodded solemnly.

"So when Laurel scared you about witches and devils and ghosts, it was really because she was frightened herself about the problems in her own family."

Marnie worked on that and nodded.

"Isn't that true, Laurel?" Mom said.

Laurel looked up and gazed past all of us. "I wanted Marnie to be safe from evil. Only true believers are saved." And her eyes were blank.

I knew it was hopeless then. Why couldn't Laurel go along with what Mom had said, at least for Marnie's sake? Couldn't Laurel give that much?

Mom turned and carried Marnie away. Diana was just coming in from the hall. "It's all right," she said to Laurel.

"What have you done?" Laurel's eyes were alive again, pinpointed on Diana. "You've done something."

"I've called Robert K. Enright from your church. He's in the phone book."

"You had no business—"

"I've told him your brother's out of control and the police are involved. I told him he'd beaten up your mother and that she's in the hospital. I told him it wasn't safe for you to go home and your dad wasn't there. I reminded him you belong to his church. And if he didn't deal with it, the community was going to hear about it."

Laurel's hand was clutching the edge of the table, frozen in place.

Diana dropped onto Mom's chair. "As a matter of fact, I told him I write for *The Suburbanite*. He's coming to get you, Laurel. You'll stay with them for the time being."

"No," Laurel said. "You've meddled. You've pushed your way into my family—"

Diana's hand came down hard on the table. "You pushed your way into *my* family." She leaned closer to Laurel.

"Diana," Dad said.

She jerked her head around at him. "Was I wrong to call her minister?"

"No," Dad said. "Just leave it at that."

"I'm going home," Laurel said, not moving.

"No," Dad said. "You aren't going to do that, Laurel."

Her hand slipped off the table. She looked younger than Marnie, and sullen. But there was something like relief in her face. Mom came back, and we sat there in silence until Robert K. Enright came.

It wasn't too long before he was there at the front

door. He'd pulled on pants and an overcoat, but he was wearing bedroom slippers.

I thought we were going to pass her to him without a word, like a hostage at a border. I was just glad she wasn't going home tonight and that she didn't have to carry everything by herself.

"We know you realize how serious this situation is," Dad said to him, just as formal as Robert K. Enright himself. "We count on you to find a safe haven for Laurel."

Mr. Enright didn't have much to say to that, though I thought we might be in for a sermon. In a regular voice he said, "I've brought my wife along. She'll drive the other car to our home." So I handed over the keys.

We watched them walk away, out of the range of the porch light. It just crossed my mind that this was still bonfire night, and I'd wanted to spend it with Laurel. And in a way I had.

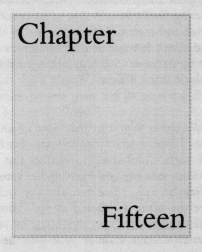

Chapter

Fifteen

Homecoming was behind us, and the bonfire was a big sooty circle out by the athletic field. The green and yellow crepe paper was off the halls. Pace Cunningham had found somebody to tape up the posters for the Fortnightly Club Christmas dance, and they were everywhere you looked.

The rumor around school was that Chance MacEnroe and C.E. were shaping up as an item, and nobody seemed particularly amazed about this except me. It was also the week Diana worked up another article to show them down at *The Suburbanite* office: "Homecoming Dance Recalls Age of Innocence."

She had some good lines in it. One of them was "While the alums doo-wopped back in time at the gym Homecoming dance on Saturday night, Founders Park, a scant block from Walden Woods High School, remained off limits to all but drug dealers and their clients."

"They'll either take it or they won't," Diana said. "Either way I'll keep submitting to them. *The Suburbanite* needs a high-school stringer, whether they know it or not." Diana was definitely getting her second wind in high school.

I got mine at the Y, where I started swimming on my own. There's no status to swimming by yourself at the Y, but you move at your own pace, and there's plenty of space around you. So I'd wind down every day in the pool. As long as you can keep afloat, a pool's a controlled environment. But I don't think I went there just because it was safe. By then I must have known there is no safe place. And swimming definitely helps me think.

One morning when Diana and I were walking to school, I was being too quiet or something.

"Laurel?" said Diana the mind-reader.

I hadn't seen her around school. "I just wonder how she's doing."

Diana kept walking. "I'm more concerned about how Marnie's doing."

"I think she's dealing with it okay. I think she's

worked it out and understands," I said, coming to Laurel's defense one last time.

"I think she understands too," Diana said, "but it's going to leave a mark on her. Things do when you're that young."

"And what about Laurel?" I said.

"You tell me."

"I suppose sooner or later her family will get back together, at least Laurel and her mother and Billy. And it'll all start up again, until Billy's old enough to do some real damage they can't cover up."

"And Laurel?" Diana said.

"Laurel will go on denying it all," I said. "Whatever happened to happy endings?"

But we were in sight of school, and Diana didn't say.

They were playing Latin rhythms over the PA between classes, and that noon I was on the way to meet C.E. for lunch.

Then I saw Laurel. She was moving through the flow of people, her books held close. Her hair was smooth, catching the light. If she'd looked scared, if she'd looked hurt, I don't know what I'd have done. But she was this perfect girl, like the first moment I'd met her.

I reached out to her and spoke her name.

"God bless you," she said, moving past me.

RICHARD PECK is the author of nineteen novels for young readers. They include the eerie adventures of Blossom Culp from Bluff City, mid-America—the author's hometown of Decatur, Illinois, somewhat disguised. He attended Exeter University in England and holds degrees from DePauw University and Southern Illinois University. His books for young readers include *Don't Look and It Won't Hurt* (recently made into the movie *Gas Food Lodging*), *Bel-Air Bambi and the Mall Rats, Unfinished Portrait of Jessica,* and *Remembering the Good Times.* His most recent book for Delacorte is an adult title, *Love and Death at the Mall: Teaching and Writing for the Literate Young.*

He is the winner of the 1990 Margaret A. Edwards Award, given by *School Library Journal* and the Young Adult Services Division of the American Library Association; the 1990 National Council of Teachers of English/ALAN Award for "outstanding contributions to young adult literature," and the 1991 Medallion from the University of Southern Mississippi, which "honors an author who has made an outstanding contribution to the field of literature."